THE STATEMENT OF STELLA MABERLY

F. Anstey was the penname of Thomas Anstey Guthrie, born in 1856. The son of a London tailor, Anstey studied to be a lawyer (though he never practised). Instead he started publishing stories in the late 1870s. He had an early 'hit' with the comic—and subsequently much-filmed— novel *Vice Versâ* (1882) in which a father and son magically change bodies for a week. (The name 'F. Anstey' is sometimes thought to be a play on the word 'fantasy'.) On the basis of this Anstey was invited to become a contributor for *Punch* by its editor F. C. Burnand and this became the centre of his literary work. *Burglar Bill* (1882) and *Mr. Punch's Model Music Hall* (1892) both appeared in the magazine. Anstey found his niche with a series of humorous novels: *The Tinted Venus* (1885), *A Fallen Idol* (1886) and *The Brass Bottle* (1900). Anstey also wrote some serious fiction: *The Pariah* (1889), about a well-off but low-born young man who tries to enter high society but encounters only disdain, and *The Statement of Stella Maberly* (1896), a psychological thriller about schizophrenia and hallucination. In later life, Anstey spent a good deal of time overseeing dramatizations of his works, and later film adaptations. Anstey had no pretensions to being seen as a 'great' author. In *A Long Retrospect* he wrote: 'my life has had no adventures, and no vicissitudes; such incidents as have happened in it have been the experiences of any author who has been fairly popular in his day and has enjoyed his work'. He died of pneumonia in 1934.

Peter Merchant is a Principal Lecturer in the School of Humanities at Canterbury Christ Church University. He is co-editor, with Catherine Waters, of a recent volume of essays on Charles Dickens, *Dickens and the Imagined Child* (Ashgate, 2015). His previous work on Anstey includes, for Victorian Secrets in 2011, an edition with full scholarly apparatus of Anstey's best-known novel *Vice Versâ*.

F. ANSTEY

THE STATEMENT OF STELLA MABERLY

Edited with an introduction and notes by
PETER MERCHANT

VALANCOURT BOOKS

Originally published by T. Fisher Unwin, London, 1896
First Valancourt Books edition 2017

Published by Valancourt Books, Richmond, Virginia
Publisher & Editor: JAMES D. JENKINS
http://www.valancourtbooks.com

ISBN 978-1-943910-61-8
Also available as an electronic book.

Set in Dante MT

CONTENTS

INTRODUCTION

In 1878, one of the happiest accidents in nineteenth-century literature thrust upon Thomas Anstey Guthrie (1856-1934) a pen name—'F. Anstey'—which the slightest of shuffles might turn into Fantasy. Soon, Anstey's breakthrough 'bodyswap' novel *Vice Versâ* (1882) was promising to make that name a positive byword for the thing of which it was so nearly an anagram. It is only because the books with which Anstey followed *Vice Versâ* were neglected (relative, at least, to the extraordinary popular success of his début) that this never happened, and not because he ever abandoned fantasy as a genre. On the contrary, that lively boyhood interest in 'magical transformations and exchanges of bodies' to which Anstey himself ascribed *Vice Versâ* would seize him again in the 1890s, and the published outcome would earn him the enthusiastic admiration of Arthur Conan Doyle.

This time, in Anstey's 1896 novel *The Statement of Stella Maberly*, the site of the exchange is different; and an altogether more sinister sort of sorcery is suggested. To the magical transformation of two male bodies that in *Vice Versâ* left the middle-aged Paul Bultitude standing helplessly in the shoes of his schoolboy son, and led to a spiralling comedy of embarrassment, there now succeeds a transformation scene in which a female body (Evelyn Heseltine's) is apparently given over to the powers of darkness. It is as if Anstey were bent on creating a literal example of the 'grotesque prestidigitation' which Thomas Hardy had recently shown Angel Clare imagining in *Tess of the d'Urbervilles* (1891). Feeling cheated of the Tess whom he knew and loved, Clare laments, 'You were one person; now you are another.' For her part, Stella Maberly—who narrates Anstey's novel—is convinced that the body of her beloved friend 'is now inhabited by a lost soul, some foul and evil spirit which has taken her form for its own vile purposes' (p. 204).

The irony here is that Stella's narrative is itself a kind of interloper too: hosted by the shell of another story whose original occupier has fled. For, demonstrably, several elements both of the narrator's 'Statement' and of the frame set around this—a frame which sees Stella, consigned by some 'mockery of mercy' to a place of permanent confinement (p. 249), seeming to reminisce from a ward in what would now be termed a secure hospital—are transferred to the novel from an earlier work that Anstey abandoned. This edition for Valancourt Books marks the first appearance in print of that earlier work, 'The Statement of V.M. patient at Bethnal House Asylum, July: 19: 1886'. It has been transcribed from a British Library manuscript not just for purposes of comparison with *The Statement of Stella Maberly* but because it is a remarkable and startling story, or piece of purported autopathography, in its own right.

'The Statement of V.M.' is written in a notebook filled with early draft versions of Anstey's works. It is strangely at variance with the surrounding material, which tends to reflect Anstey's public image as a humorist (at that time being paid four guineas a week by the comic magazine *Punch*). The work appears to have been done at the end of 1888, in early December, so there is a slight chronological gap between the date of composition and the date which is set to the supposed statement. The backdating of the latter to the summer of 1886 is explained by the manuscript's heading, which lists 'Dr Miller & Dr Will' as among the asylum staff to whom V.M.'s statement is made. It had indeed been in 1886 that John Kennedy Will succeeded John Millar as medical superintendent of London's Bethnal House Asylum. Anstey evidently wanted to add accuracy and authenticity by naming the current incumbent, but felt at the same time that he owed it to George Millar—his sister's husband and his own longtime friend—to pay what by now was posthumous tribute to George's father by also putting, albeit with one discreetly altered vowel, that surname in the frame.

Not only had Anstey in the spring of 1882 stayed with the Millars at Bethnal House, as we know from his autobiography *A Long Retrospect*, but at the very time he committed 'The Statement of V.M.' to his notebook his younger brother Leonard was securing—at the Paddington Green Children's Hospital and the Regent's Park Hospital for Epilepsy, Paralysis, and other Diseases of the Nervous System—the first appointments of a very distinguished career in neurology and paediatrics. In addition to the access which Anstey thereby earned to specialist psycho-medical knowledge, he had acquired by December 1888 some unwanted and distressing first-hand experience. Anstey's father (or 'P.' for 'Pater') was by that time in the final months of his life, and increasingly confused, so that Anstey's entries in his diary for 1888 include the following: '16: Nov. P. complaining that he was continually fancying himself in a strange house'; '25: Nov. P. gloomy again—inclined to self-accusation.'

From what Anstey had necessarily begun to hear and see of nervous disease and delusions, it was a short step to the disordered thinking and possibly distorted memories which inform the statement of 'V.M.' She speaks of mysterious voices that seem to whisper 'Hidden Children' to her, and in a railway tunnel outside Croydon she imagines the engine plunging into the centre of the earth and 'that great monster dragging me with others down to an unknown world perhaps to Hell'. (Here, Anstey is on the same terrifying track as Anna Kingsford with her 'Doomed Train', the first item in Kingsford's just-published collection of *Dreams and Dream-Stories*.) There are hallucinatory visions of the damned and haunting flashbacks to traumatic past episodes: the deaths of her first husband, 'Capt. W. Mackeith,' and of their daughter; a murderous attack on another woman by the seaside. Nothing resembling these torments or these rages had been in Anstey's range before. 'V.' stands for Violet, but—threatening her second husband with a meat cleaver, and admitting 'a strong desire to take to smashing things'—this Violet is certainly not for shrinking. What the text ultimately leaves open is whether she has been driven to so dangerous an edge by a deeply troubled mind or a troubled second marriage. Her unnamed second husband, a music teacher, may have conspired with a Doctor whose name is also undisclosed to have her declared insane: 'My husband & he great friends. Easy to have me sent to an Asylum.' That the Victorians used diagnoses of madness to manage mutinous women is a conclusion often reached by social historians today, but to find such suspicions voiced by the Victorians themselves is rare. If Anstey means them to be given any credence, then marriage rather than Bethnal House Asylum is the institution in which Violet M. has found herself restrained; and her so-called madness is less a psychological condition than a specific cultural infliction. She is one of those man-made volcanoes with which not many male Victorian novelists ventured to challenge male complacency. As George Meredith has the heroine of *Diana of the Crossways* (1885) reflect, with Krakatoa much in mind, 'They [men] create by stoppage a volcano, and are amazed at its eruptiveness.'

At some stage during the winter of 1894-95, Anstey returned to 'The Statement of V.M.' and in a notebook now held by the British Library made the synopsis which the present edition reproduces after the story proper. This résumé of what is now represented as a Millar's tale (that name having passed peculiarly from physician to patient) served to remind Anstey of the incidents which he had invented, and the problems which he had posed, six years earlier. The reason he wanted a reminder was that he was now considering how, with an extra measure of elbow-room, he might engineer a fiction identically framed; and this was the single-volume novel, as it became when published in the spring of 1896, which would have as its title *The Statement of Stella Maberly*. Anstey's diary entries for 1895 duly record: '14: Jan. First idea of 'Stella Maberly.' 15th Began outline ... 3: April. Began 'Stella Maberly' ... 14: Dec. 'Statement of Stella Maberly' finished & sent to Fisher Unwin.' Anstey's recourse to this publisher, for whose 1886 *Annual* (a portmanteau volume put together by Henry Norman and entitled *The Broken Shaft: Tales in Mid-Ocean*) he had already supplied a story of haunting, may measure his sense of the difference between the painful psychic interiors of 'The Statement of V.M.' and the tale of out-and-out supernatural terror into which—seven years later—that study of 'the awful frienzy [*sic*] of a maddened brain' was threatening to turn. For there was to be a transformation scene embedded in *The Statement of Stella Maberly*, to make the novel pivot upon what it would invite its reader to construe as a case of full-blown demonic possession.

At least, for reasons which it is necessary at this point to tease out a little more, that becomes what the second and subsequent editions invite. Initially, there is a complicating factor already present in the novel's unpublished precursor. As is of course indicated by the 'Statement of' pattern into which both titles fall, the subject of each story is also its narrator; and Stella, like Violet, is volatile, fanciful, prone to nervous breakdowns, the very definition of unreliable. We cannot know whether to regard her perceptions as true or mistrust them as delusions arising from that grey area in late nineteenth-century mental science where neurology and psychiatry overlap. Stella's own conviction that demonology holds the key to the plot is countered in Chapter 8 by Canon Broadbent's insistence that Stella is suffering from those staples of the Victorian sensation novel, 'ill-health, a disordered imagination, overwrought nerves' (p. 205) and 'mental agitation' (p. 207), and that it is therefore psychological medicine which must solve the mystery. Crucially, Fisher Unwin encouraged this view by not crediting *The Statement of Stella Maberly* to Anstey at all at first but publishing it, at the end of March 1896, as 'Written by Herself'. The book was asking its readers to take it as a madness memoir, and so to look in it for the sort of 'morbid hallucinations' (p. 161) which might illustrate the narrator's increasing detachment from reality. It is no wonder that most reviewers of *The Statement of Stella Maberly* sided with the Canon. Rather than taking the incidents which the narrative recounts as pointers to demonic possession, the reviewers advised, readers should consider them 'hallucinations of Stella's as her madness increases' (*Saturday Review*, 5 September 1896). So what the book offers is 'a curious portrayal of the neurotic temperament' (*Leeds Mercury*, 1 June 1896) or 'merely a mad story about a madwoman, who takes it into her head that an evil spirit is occupying her friend's body' (*Pall Mall Gazette*, 13 May 1896).

After six months, however, that 'Written by Herself' label which had made this 'a mad story' was superseded by the publisher's belated identification of Anstey as the author. What earlier in the year had had to be read as a psychological case history, whether faithful to the facts or fabricated, could now be read as a carefully crafted thriller about demonic possession. The physician might still see 'a perfect picture of ... a paranoiac [led] to a violent deed', as Smith Ely Jelliffe put it in the *New York*

Journal of Nervous and Mental Disease (November 1897); but lay readers could approach the book as based on a strong storyline idea suggested by the spirit world, rather than on professional or personal knowledge of a mind diseased. *The Statement of Stella Maberly* became, potentially, as much a Gothic encounter with embodied evil as a curious portrayal of the neurotic (or neurasthenic) temperament. The balance that Anstey was able to strike between those competing possibilities is indeed a hallmark of the book's period, the 1890s. Situated both by date and by inclination midway between the psychological insights of Charlotte Perkins Gilman's 'The Yellow Wallpaper' (1892) and the supernatural frissons of Bram Stoker's *Dracula* (1897), Anstey's novel seems to take some tincture of each.

Since the 1880s, in fact, Anstey had counted Stoker and his wife as friends; and on 17 February 1895, with *Stella Maberly* just starting to take shape and a good deal of material already gathered for *Dracula*, they met for Sunday lunch. Each man's work-in-progress positively reinforced the interest of the other in concentrating his resources upon the recently resurgent literary Gothic and in developing the powerful binaries of Stevenson's *Strange Case of Dr Jekyll and Mr Hyde* (1886) and Wilde's *Picture of Dorian Gray* (1890). For Anstey, this would entail creating within the 'Statement' a second character whose presence might promote the exploration of the divided self and permit a pitting of good against evil. So he couples Stella, who descends from Violet, with Stella's cherished childhood friend, Evelyn Heseltine, for whom 'The Statement of V.M.' had contained no counterpart and in whom thanks simply to Anstey's choice of forename, 'Evelyn,' 'evil' is already phonetically present. From an admirer of Walter Scott's *Tales of the Crusaders*—such as Anstey had already shown himself to be—the choice of that name might already be a declaration of plotting intent. Scott's novel *The Betrothed* (1825) had a heroine called Eveline to whom 'it often seemed … as if a good and evil power strove for mastery over her destiny'. She is protected by a portrait of the Virgin Mary which seems to come to life; but she is also threatened in her bed by the phantom Vanda; and both the 'benign saint' and the 'vindictive fiend' then feature in her dreams.

The oppositional female types thus placed either side of Scott's Eveline come of course from the stock cupboard of fantasy fiction. But it is significant that Anstey raids it too, to make them the basic building blocks of his design for *The Statement of Stella Maberly*. One kind of reading of Anstey's novel, the kind completely coloured by the assumption of a Stella who is criminally insane, would see the vindictive femme fatale as stalking the blessed virgin from the first and even as killing her. Stella may not be so 'guiltless' with regard to the phial of chloral as she claims (p. 89); and the strangling to which the narrative leads up is either an act of murderous malice cunningly passed off as self-defence or, at best, testimony to the massive misconstruction—seeing the fiend in the friend—that Stella's 'perverted imaginings' (p. 219) have produced. On this view, Evelyn is fragile, innocent, and angelic while Stella is the dangerously unhinged dark destroyer. Maurice Greiffenhagen's frontispiece illustration for the first edition portrays exactly this; the figure on the left is 'fair, with a delicate, spiritual beauty which corresponded to her gentle nature' (p. 9); and presents a marked contrast to the figure on the right, a young woman with an 'oval, olive-tinted face' and a 'crown of soft dark hair' (p. 52). If however the novel is read supernaturally, as a story of demonic possession in which the Fair Maiden is turned overnight into a Dark Lady, the ingénue and the vindictive femme fatale are not Evelyn and Stella but (respectively) the Evelyn of Chapters 1 to 4 and the Evelyn of Chapters 5 to 9. At the start of the fifth chapter Evelyn dies as one woman, to return as quite another. Instead of one of the heroines being pure while the other is crazed and predatory, both of those extremes (together with most of the contradictions which define the destiny of Scott's Eveline, 'Widow'd wife and wedded maid, / Betrothed, betrayer, and betray'd') meet and are realised in Evelyn alone.

It took Anstey not six months but fully twenty years to give that supernatural reading his direct and explicit authorial sanction. In February 1916 he turned the novel into a 'scenario' for a silent movie entitled 'An Evil Spirit'. The film was never made but aimed to do all that its title promises, dealing in an avowedly weird and fantastic fashion with the subject of demonic possession. A full transcription of this previously unknown scenario, taken from another British Library manuscript, is added in the present edition to the text of the novel itself. It will be seen that the scenario restores to the frame story of the woman who ends in a criminal lunatic asylum the prominence it had had in 'The Statement of V.M.', while the inner story on the other hand (which necessarily unfolds in flashbacks) owes more to *The Statement of Stella Maberly*. The scenario goes beyond the novel, however, in underlining the contrast between Evelyn's 'sweetness & innocence' before the transformation and her malevolence afterwards. That 'wicked, beautiful face' (p. 244) which for Stella in the novel plainly belongs to 'a fiend in human form' (p. 243) taking possession of her friend's 'lifeless shell' (p. 168) was to be made visible on the screen at the moment of entry, when Evelyn 'dies' for the first time, as well as at the exit point, when Evelyn dies definitively.

It is clear that with 'The Statement of V.M.', *The Statement of Stella Maberly*, and 'An Evil Spirit' Anstey moved into territory far removed from *Vice Versâ*. In the last of the three, planned and executed as he approached his sixtieth birthday, he seized the possibilities of the new cinematic medium while other writers of his generation were ignoring them. In the first and the second he broke new ground with his serious attempt to connect fiction to psychomedical discourse, and by subscribing to that unusual gender-crossing manoeuvre in which a male author disappears inside a female narrator. Individually considered, the story, the novel, and the scenario all deserve to be better known. Collectively considered, they plead strongly for increased critical attention henceforward to the shelfload of surprises, here and elsewhere, which their author has in readiness.

Peter Merchant
October 2016

NOTE ON THE TEXTS

The text used for *The Statement of Stella Maberly* is that of the first UK edition (1896), published without the name of the author. This edition contained a handful of minor misprints, which in line with Anstey's obvious intentions are silently corrected here.

The rest of the material is transcribed from manuscripts held in the collection of the British Library, and I am grateful to the Library and its staff for the access which I have had to these. The catalogue numbers of the notebooks containing the relevant items are as follows:

> for 'The Statement of V.M. patient at Bethnal House Asylum, July: 19: 1886', Additional MS 54278 (this notebook carries an index, prepared by Anstey himself, which abbreviates the title of the work as 'Statement of V.M. a Lunatic');

> for 'Violet Millar's Tale', the résumé of 'The Statement of V.M.' which was made in the winter of 1894-95, Additional MS 54283;

> for the scenario 'An Evil Spirit', Additional MS 54308.

In each of these transcriptions, the numbers of the folio sheets on which successive portions of the text appear are indicated within square brackets. The first two of the three texts transcribed use reverse numbering although in the third the numbering is straightforward. Anstey would often number the manuscript pages of a story in a descending sequence, since he tended to flip his notebooks over and work inwards from the back as well as from the front; and he would sometimes skip pages, apparently leaving a space for some shorter piece on which he was simultaneously engaged. 'The Statement of V.M.' follows this pattern and therefore has a backward-directed page range, running from fo. (for folio) 127v to fo. 107r.

The technical presentation of the scenario has been tidied by the occasional restoration of a heading such as 'Leader' or an instruction such as 'Fade into' which Anstey forgot, although the less easily adjusted irregularities (as when he uses one of the scene numbers—58—twice over, or lifts the 'Action' up into the 'Scene') have been allowed to stand. Editing has otherwise been kept to a minimum, with all editorial interventions indicated within square or triangular brackets and italicized. So an editorial '[sic]' denotes an error which Anstey apparently neither intended nor noticed. The parenthesized '(sic)' which twice appears in 'The Statement of V.M.', on fos 126v and 116r, is different; these two insertions are Anstey's own, designed to show that he is aware of spelling errors in the narrative he is purportedly copying (the narrator ends her 'Statement' with an apology for its 'many mistakes & scratchings').

Where there is something illegible in Anstey's manuscript, '<word?>' has been used to mark the enforced omission; at any points in the transcription process where certainty has had to give way to surmise, a '<?>' has been added which shows that the reading given is conjectural. Where Anstey abbreviates words, the missing letters have been restored, in order to avoid giving the text the appearance of a coded message; and full stops have also been inserted where sentences needed to be separated. No other additional punctuation has been applied.

In the transcribed text of 'The Statement of V.M.', Anstey's deletions and overwritings, which often illuminate his thought process, are indicated with strikethroughs. Authorial deletions in the manuscript of 'An Evil Spirit' are similarly marked wherever a change of mind is or might be involved, rather than a simple slip of the pen. There are no authorial deletions in the résumé entitled 'Violet Millar's Tale'.

For a more detailed account of the texts contained in this edition, see Peter Merchant, "Thomas Anstey Guthrie's Madness Shuffle: Steps toward a Nightmare Scenario," *Nineteenth-Century Theatre and Film* 42 (2015): 146-163.

THE STATEMENT OF STELLA MABERLY

PRELIMINARY NOTE

THE manuscript of this book was placed in my hands with an express stipulation that I should not reveal the writer's identity until, or unless I received authority to do so.

Should the narrative excite the interest and sympathy I anticipate for it, I may be permitted, later on, to disclose certain facts connected with its origin which the friends of 'Stella Maberly' think it advisable, for many reasons, to withhold for the present.

In any case, I consider her Statement strange and striking enough to attract attention for its own sake—or, naturally, I should not have undertaken to publish it under the circumstances.

T. FISHER UNWIN.

INTRODUCTION

I, STELLA MABERLY, have determined to make a full statement of all the circumstances in my life which led me to commit an act that, in itself, would seem a crime deserving of nothing but condemnation.

I shall write it rather for my own satisfaction than that of others, for there may come a time when, as has been the case before, my memory grows confused and I begin to wonder whether, after all, I may not have been mistaken, and, what is more dreadful still, to doubt whether I am not actually as guilty as I have been made to appear.

So, while my recollection is still vivid and clear, I am going to put everything down on paper as accurately and impartially as I can, so that if, in the future, these horrible doubts should again assail me, I shall be able, simply by reading this statement, to see exactly what I did and the reasons I had for doing it.

After I am gone I should like others to read it too. Probably very few will believe that what I am writing is the truth; but that will not matter to me then, and even already I have ceased to care very much what the world outside may think.

Still, it pleases me to fancy that, perhaps here and there, someone who knew me once will read this and believe that it is just possible that poor Stella Maberly was more to be pitied than blamed.

I shall begin my statement with some account of my childhood, not because it was eventful or interesting, but because, without it, much that followed would seem less intelligible and excusable.

The Statement of Stella Maberly

I

I have no recollection of my mother, although she did not die until I was nearly four years old. She and my father separated shortly after I was born, and remained apart till her death. She was extremely beautiful, as I know from a portrait that exists of her, but cursed, I believe, with so violent a temper that it soon became impossible to live with her. Where or how she died I don't know, for my father was always reserved on the subject, even when I was old enough to ask questions about her; but I can just remember the news coming that she was dead, and my nurse pulling down the nursery blinds and telling me I had lost my poor mamma and should have to wear black frocks.

I cried bitterly, not because I understood my loss in the least, but because I hated dark rooms and being dressed in black.

Within a year my father married again, and was much happier in his second marriage than I fear he could ever have been in his first. My stepmother was not unkind; I think she was prepared to treat me with as much affection as a child of her own, if I had responded at all to her advances. But she did not understand me; I was a difficult child to deal with, possessed as I was, at times, by twin demons of jealousy and sullenness, which made me resist all her endearments. Possibly I was encouraged in this antagonism by my own nurse, who was devoted to me, and resented, as such servants are apt to do, the fact that my importance was diminished by my father having taken a new wife, and by the second family that came in time.

Between my half-brothers and sisters and myself their mother never permitted herself to make distinctions, or, if she did, it was in my favour, for she treated my outbreaks of defiance with more leniency than she would probably have shown to them had they ever been capable of such rebellious rages as I flew into on little or no provocation, so violent that they left me, when their force was spent, weak and exhausted for hours afterwards.

Once I recall my father saying, half to himself, and with a suppressed groan, when, as a last resource, I had been brought before him for reproof, 'God grant she may not grow up like her mother!' which puzzled me, for my mother seemed to me, from her picture, very lovely. I know now that he was thinking of the want of self-control which had wrecked her happiness and his.

As I grew older, these outbursts became less violent, or rather took the form of sullen and prolonged silences, during which I rejected all overtures, and even went without food for hours and hours, to the distress and bewilderment of the younger children, who were too sweet-natured to comprehend an anger which lasted so long after its occasion.

And yet, in the very worst of these black moods of mine, my heart was secretly aching to own myself in the wrong and be forgiven and accept the love I knew was waiting for me—but I could not. I seemed to be in the grip of some paralysing force which would not relax by any effort of my own will, which made me hard and cruel in spite of my self.

With a temperament like this, it might have been expected that I should grow up a sickly, puny little creature, as unloved as I made myself unlovable—but it was not so. I had a physique too strong to be affected by my fits of passion and brooding; I was healthy and vigorous, fond of exercise and open air, with mental abilities that, when I chose to exert them, were rather above than below the average. And when my demons were not aroused I was a natural, bright, impulsively demonstrative child, who could both feel and attract affection.

My half-brothers and sisters adored me, and were my admiring little slaves as long as I chose to tyrannise over them; the servants would do more for me than for any of the other children; the governesses I had—though I made their lives so unendurable that not one of them could stand the strain for more than a few months—even they broke down when they had to leave, and confessed that they felt the parting as bitterly as if I had been the best of pupils. I daresay they went away thinking me harder and more

heartless than ever, as I remained passive and dry-eyed throughout the leave-taking; they did not know—I took care that no one
should know—that when my governess had driven away for ever
I would steal up into a box room at the top of the house and set
myself to recall every cruel and insulting speech of mine to her,
and every instance of affection and forbearance she had shown
me until my heart swelled with contrition and I found that I, too,
could weep—when weeping was of no use.

And yet—in spite of all my good resolutions—I would be just
as perverse and wilful and unmanageable to the next governess
that undertook to instruct me as to her predecessor.

This state of things could not go on; I had wearied out any
affection my stepmother ever felt for me, and she was afraid of
the example my insubordination might set to her own children
—or so she persuaded my father—and it was decided that I must
be sent away to school.

The school that was chosen for me was a fashionable and
expensive establishment at one of the best known seaside towns.
It was excellently conducted; the principal was an able and cultivated woman, who took a real interest in the mental and moral
training of every pupil. She was a firm disciplinarian, and for the
first time I found myself under an authority which I could not
defy with impunity. I took some pains to please her, and in time,
though I often vexed and disappointed her, she came to feel a certain fondness for me.

My schoolfellows all belonged to the well-born and well-to-do
class, and received me readily enough into their friendship; they
were mostly pleasant, simple-minded girls, and there were few
of them I actually disliked, though fewer still with whom I was
really intimate.

Still, I was very far from unpopular; in fact, I soon found
myself the unwilling object of a sort of cult. I had the kind of
irregular beauty, the cleverness and audacity which girls admire
in another, and I had, too, the crowning charm of uncertainty
and caprice.

Up to a certain age girls are frequently great heroine worshippers, and whether they transfer their idolatry later to one of the
opposite sex or not, it is always rather increased than checked by

being trampled upon. They adored me none the less for being disdainful and imperious.

I am afraid I took a morbid pleasure in wounding or quarrelling with the friends I loved best for the mere emotional luxury of feeling miserable and alone and misunderstood, and I knew that they would always be only too delighted to be taken back into my favour.

Perhaps all this may sound like conceit or arrogance—but I shall let it stand. I am far enough from feeling even a retrospective vanity, and such attractions as I possess, or may have once possessed, have brought me small satisfaction, as will be seen before I reach the conclusion of my story.

I had one rival in the school who, curiously enough perhaps, was the only girl there for whom I felt anything like deep affection, and whom, characteristically, I treated with most unkindness. Her name was Evelyn Heseltine; she was an orphan and would, it was vaguely understood, be immensely wealthy when she came of age.

She was utterly unlike me in every respect; fair, with a delicate, spiritual beauty which corresponded to her gentle nature, incapable of an ill-natured speech or an ungenerous thought. It was a favourite device of my enemies—for I need scarcely say that I had enemies—to attempt to mortify me by declaring her to be by far the loveliest and cleverest girl in the school, but in this amiable design they failed, for even I could not be jealous of Evelyn, perhaps because I felt that my superiority was never seriously questioned.

I took the lead in all our amusements, in all our innocent scrapes or festivities; in our riding-school parties on the Downs it was I who was always given the most spirited mounts; in the class-rooms Evelyn had slightly the advantage, but she was naturally the more industrious, and, even at work, I could outshine her whenever I chose to take the trouble.

She was not strong enough to excel in sports or games; timid and sensitive, but with a disposition so sweet that it was next to impossible to provoke her into a quarrel or even a retort, which often exasperated me into making cruel experiments upon her powers of forbearance. She had too much character, nevertheless, to be charged with insipidity, though even her strongest supporters confessed that she wanted one thing to be absolutely perfect—a spice of the devil.

And, even when I was most cruel, I loved her; I felt instinctively that hers was a pure and noble influence, and I had the grace to be proud of her attachment to me, though, with my old self-tormenting impulse, I trifled with it until I was in danger of losing it altogether. But Evelyn always understood, and bore with and pitied me up to the very end.

I do not know how other women may regard their school days, but I look back upon mine as the happiest part of a life which, it is true, has not been either long or happy, and I was sorry rather than glad when they came to an end and I returned home, as I thought, for good.

For a while after I had 'come out,'[1] and was entitled to take my part in such social events as were provided by the rather dull Hampshire neighbourhood in which we lived, I found existence fairly enjoyable. People made much of me, and seemed glad to secure me for dinners and dances and garden-parties; my father was proud of my success, and indulged me in every wish; I had my train of admirers, more than one of whom did me the honour of proposing for my hand, but none of them touched my heart.

They were the ordinary, well-groomed, sport-loving young Englishmen, not by any means intellectual, and who, under the influence of sentiment, seemed more stupid than they really were. I found them only a degree less wearisome than I had the silliest of my schoolgirl worshippers, and treated them with much the same merciless ridicule, so that I soon earned a reputation in the county for heartlessness.

I do not think I was more heartless than any other girl who is critical and fastidious, and who has never met the man who answers at all to her secret ideal, but there seemed to me something at once absurd and irritating in the spectacle of a passion I had never cared to inspire, and could not return, and this prevented me from feeling or showing any sign of pity.

Gradually, almost imperceptibly at first, I became aware that my popularity was declining. I found chilly greetings and hostile looks at several houses where I had once been eagerly welcomed. I was made to feel, by innumerable indications, slight but unmistakable, that I had given offence and was out of favour. This distressed me very little; I had soon tired of the neighbours around us and was glad of the excuse for indulging my growing distaste for society. So by degrees I gave up going out; lived almost entirely to myself, and took all my rides and walks alone, and in directions where I was least likely to meet acquaintances. This passion for solitude in a young woman of my age and position no doubt seemed unnatural, and formed a fruitful subject for local gossip—but to that I was perfectly indifferent.

However, it served to make my home-life almost unendurable, for my stepmother, as I had begun to see of late, was secretly jealous of the preference my father showed for me, and the change in my habits gave her a pretext for coming between us which she was not likely to neglect. I was forbidden to ride or walk without an escort, as though I had been a child, and my half-brothers and sisters were instructed to accompany me and act as spies, which I need not say destroyed any vestige of affection I felt towards them.

Now that he could no longer take any pride in my social successes, my father was easily influenced against me; he expressed strong disapproval of my solitary pursuits, and attempted to force me to go into society as I used to do, for he insisted that the slights and rebuffs which made the effort so impossible to me were exaggerated, if not purely fanciful—as if my powers of perception were not likely to be keener than his in matters which concerned me so closely.

I yielded to his wishes to some extent, only to encounter further mortifications, which cut me to the quick, though pride forbade me to betray it. I grew more and more unhappy and restless, and should have been utterly miserable if I had not found some distraction in writing.

I had always had an ambition to be an author, and I wrote one or two short stories with a facility and fluency that gave me the hope of having found my vocation in life.

The hope proved delusive; my manuscripts returned to me again and again; some editors admitted that they showed some fancy and imagination, but were too crude and inexperienced to be worthy of acceptance. I flung them into the fire at last in a fit of temper, and sullenly recognised that, though I might be at least as well-educated and original as some of the women-writers who have sprung into popularity, literary distinction was not for me. I might persevere, of course, but the glow and the confidence had departed; it did not seem worth while to court any further failures.

And then something happened which turned my thoughts into a different channel altogether. One day my stepmother sent for me to her boudoir and told me that my father had just received news of the failure of a bank in Australia in which he was a large shareholder. What his liabilities were exactly he did not know as yet, but the greatest economy would be necessary if we were even to go on living in our present home; the horses and carriages must be sold, and we must all learn to do without the luxuries we had been accustomed to.

She ended by suggesting that I should rouse myself from what she was pleased to call my 'selfish isolation,' and make some return for the expensive education I had been given, by helping to teach my youngest sister and saving the cost of a governess.

All this was said with an insidious show of affection which did not deceive me in the least. I knew perfectly well that she hoped to provoke me into some protest against such humiliation as the position of unpaid drudge in my own father's household. I saw, too, that, even if I accepted the task, she would take care that I did not succeed in it—she meant to drive me out of my home, and out of my father's heart as well, if she could.

So I answered that I quite understood that I was an encumbrance to them all, and that I ought in future to support myself; but, as to doing so by the means she suggested, she must be aware that the relations between her children and myself put that quite out of the question, as she herself had completely destroyed any influence I might once have had over them.

And with that I left her and wrote at once to my old school-mistress, recalling myself to her, explaining that I found myself compelled by family circumstances to go out into the world and earn my bread, and asking her if she knew anyone to whom she could recommend me as a governess.

I had an answer within two days. The letter began by an assurance that the writer remembered me perfectly, and was sorry to hear of the change in my prospects. From what she recollected of my temperament a few years ago, she doubted whether I was fitted for so trying a life as a governess's—but it so happened that a pleasanter and easier position might possibly be obtained if I cared to apply for it.

The day before my letter arrived she had had a visit from a former pupil of hers and old school-fellow of mine, Evelyn Heseltine, who had just returned to England after having been abroad for her health during the past few years. She was now recovered and intended to occupy a house in Surrey that belonged to her, and had mentioned her desire to find a companion of about her own age who would come and live with her there. Evelyn had asked most affectionately after me, and the writer felt sure that she would be overjoyed at securing the companionship of her old friend and school-fellow if possible.

I had seen nothing of Evelyn since our school-days, though we had corresponded for a time. After she went abroad our letters had gradually ceased, and I had almost forgotten her existence till the letter reminded me of it. Now all the old times came back with a rush; I remembered Evelyn's goodness and sweetness, and felt a great longing to see her again. She used to care for me—perhaps cared for me still—and I felt so alone and unloved at home.

It seemed almost too good to be true that she and I might really be together again, that I should leave the jangle and worry of home life, not for slavery amongst strangers, but a quiet and peaceful existence with the dearest friend I had ever had—the one friend I had left in the whole world now.

I wrote to Evelyn that night, as the principal had given me her address in Surrey, and shortly after received an enthusiastic reply. Nothing could be more fortunate, I was the very person she would have most wished for; I was to come as soon as possible, and she would do everything she could to make me happy.

So I was able to forestall my stepmother's intentions, and leave home of my own free will; not without some opposition from my father, it is true, though he gave way when he saw that I was determined to carry my point. And here I will stop for the present, having arrived at the stage where my story may really be said to begin.

II

The day arrived on which I was to enter upon my new life, and, during the tedious cross-country journey from my Hampshire home to the little village near the border of Kent and Surrey that was my destination, I had ample time for misgivings.

Should I find Evelyn Heseltine the same as she was four years ago? Would she be quite unspoilt by wealth, quite unaffected by the relations of patroness and dependent that were now to exist between us? True, I could detect no shade of patronage in her letter, but she might betray it in her manner, notwithstanding.

She had arranged to meet me at the station, and any doubts I had were dispelled the moment I had alighted on the whinstone platform and saw her coming eagerly towards me.

I can see her still; tall and slender in the fawn-coloured serge, pale pink shirt, and small sailor hat, which were being worn that season; her soft hazel eyes shining with pleasure and welcome, her cheeks flushed with a delicate rose, and her bright hair slightly ruffled by the May breeze.

Yes, she was unchanged, except that her former air of diffidence and timidity had been replaced by the ease and self-possession which a few years' experience of the world will give to the most unassuming. Even before she spoke my name with glad recognition, and our hands met, I knew that she loved me as dearly as ever, and the joy and relief I felt almost prevented me from speaking.

We were soon seated in the carriage with the pair of smart ponies which Evelyn drove herself, and as she had told the groom to follow behind with the luggage-cart, we were able to talk freely.

'It's so delightful to have you here, Stella,' she said as soon as the ponies required less of her attention; 'and you are so exactly what I hoped you would be, only even more—but I forgot, you always hated to be told about your looks, didn't you?'

'Did I?' I said. 'At all events, I'm glad *you* approve of me; and if we must talk about one another's appearance, you are looking wonderfully well, Evelyn, far stronger than ever you promised to be. I was afraid, from Mrs Chichester's letter, that you were still delicate.'

'I feel perfectly well just now,' she answered; 'there was nothing seriously the matter with me, only the doctors said I had a weak heart. I suppose I outgrew my strength at school; at all events, they said I ought to live abroad for a time and avoid worry and excitement. I should have come home long ago, only I liked the life in Italy so; and no one can accuse existence here of being dangerously exciting—I'm only afraid you will find it dull.'

I protested with perfect sincerity that I should be quite contented if I never saw a strange face, and that I wanted no society but hers.

'It's not quite so bad as that!' she exclaimed, laughing. 'My aunt, Mrs Maitland, is living at Tansted with us. We must have a chaperon of some sort; and, of course, there are people about who seem pleasant and friendly, and we shall have to see something of them. And the country is perfectly lovely; you and I will ride and drive every day when it's fine, and if we have to stay indoors we shall find plenty of things to do—music and books and work. You must try not to be bored while you are with me, though I'm afraid I sha'n't keep you very long.'

'If it depends on me,' I said, 'I am not at all likely to wish to leave you. Why do you think I should?'

'Oh, because—' she replied, 'because, of course, I shall have to give you up to somebody sooner or later, Stella. You are much too beautiful not to be fallen in love with. Perhaps, even now, there is someone who—you won't mind telling me if there is, and then, when the time *does* come, I shall feel more prepared.'

'There is nobody,' I said. 'I have had one or two offers of marriage, but I never cared enough for any man yet to give up my life to him, and I don't believe I ever shall.'

'Your heart will be touched some day,' said Evelyn. 'Then you will speak differently.'

'I doubt it,' I replied. 'I don't think my heart is capable of that kind of sentiment. Some women are born with no vocation for marriage, and I believe I am one of them. And really,' I added, 'if we are to be separated by one of us marrying, *I* am hardly the most likely person to be chosen.'

'Indeed, you are wrong, Stella, if you mean that it is I,' said Evelyn. 'I made up my mind before I came home—when we were in Italy—that I would never think of marrying unless I was sure—of what I never can be perfectly certain of now. But how silly of us to be anticipating parting when we have only just met! It seems so wonderful our coming together like this, Stella. It was the merest accident that I told dear old Mrs Chichester about my wanting to find somebody about my own age to come and live with me. I hardly expected she would know of any one. And if I had, I never dreamed for a moment that *you* of all people in the world—'

'Would have been obliged to try to earn my own living,' I said, as she left the sentence uncompleted. '*I* thought it unlikely enough once. But my father lost most of his money, and my stepmother made me so miserable at home—I had no choice.'

'You poor Stella!' exclaimed Evelyn, tenderly. 'What a trial it must have been for you! But you don't mind now you have come to me, do you? It isn't as if you were with strangers. Tansted is to be your real home now, as long as ever you care to make it so.'

And my heart grew lighter and lighter as we drove on through the pretty Surrey landscape, under the horse chestnut trees with their tossing, creamy plumes, past cottage gardens and orchards where the fruit trees spread their branches, laden with rose-flushed snow, against the pure blue of the sky, and the air was sweet with hawthorn and the fragrant gums of pines and larches.

Presently we turned off the road, through a gateway and under an ivy-covered arch, after which I saw my future home for the first time. Tansted House was a delightful old Tudor or Caroline mansion—I forget which—with barge boarded gables and herring-bone brickwork filling up the spaces of the half-timbered upper story, which projected and was supported by carved corbels. It was not large—even with the additions that had been built some time in this century. I had a glimpse, as I entered, of long, low-ceilinged rooms with spacious latticed windows, an impression of old-world *pot-pourri*, mingled with the delicate scent of azaleas and the freshness of garden flowers, and then Evelyn took me up at once to a pretty chintz-hung bedroom opposite her own.

'This is to be your room, Stella,' she said. 'I do so hope you will like it. I want you so much to feel comfortable and at home here.' And she left me to rest after the journey, with an affectionate embrace and repeated assurances of her delight in having me with her.

After she had gone I went to the window and stood looking out on the velvet lawn below, with the fine old cedar, ringed by a circular seat of faded blue; from the tiled roof over my head came the sleepy crooning and 'roo-coo-hooing' of pigeons; in the garden, beyond the lawn, a whip-lash fountain[2] pattered and tinkled musically as the breeze drove its spray this way and that.

It was all so restful and sweet, such a haven of refuge for my wounded and troubled mind. It filled me with a great peace, a soothing sense of security. Here, at least, the black moods of depression and sullenness would have no power over me, no hateful suspicions could find lodgment now I had shaken off the demons which had made my life a burden. With such a home and such a friend, how could even I be anything but happy?

I should have been insensible indeed if I had been unmoved by this, and if my heart had not been lifted up just then by a passion of love and gratitude towards her to whom I owed so much more than I could ever repay. I would, I vowed to myself, be worthy of her goodness. By no act or word of mine would I ever grieve that gentle nature. No friend Evelyn might have chosen could be more loyal and devoted than I would prove myself.

Not a difficult resolve to make or keep for anyone of ordinary good feeling, it will be thought. And yet I was destined to find it hard enough, as those who have sufficient patience to follow my unhappy story will discover before very long.

Sometimes I wonder whether, by any effort of mine, I could have overcome my nature altogether for long, and how far our thoughts and feelings really are within our own control, as we are so often told they are. I only know that these good intentions of mine were absolutely sincere at the time, and indeed I honestly believe that I carried them out as faithfully as was possible to such a temperament as mine. Perhaps, if things had only happened differently, I should never—but it is idle to speculate on what might have been, and I must return to actual facts.

When I went downstairs again, I was presented to Mrs Maitland, the aunt of whom Evelyn had spoken. She was a widow of about fifty, pleasant to look upon, with a manner which, though kindly and amiable, was somewhat fussy and over-anxious, and, as I soon discovered, without an idea that was not absolutely safe and commonplace.

I might have expected that she would look upon me as a rival and treat me with a certain reserve, if not with suppressed hostility, but her greeting was as cordial as it was obviously sincere.

'So nice for dear Evelyn to have someone of her own age about her, my dear Miss Maberly!' she remarked. 'I'm sure I often felt, while we were abroad together, what a poor companion I was, for I'm too old and stupid to take the interest she does in things; in *my* young days girls weren't as highly educated as they are now, and I never *was* clever. And now we're at Tansted, there's so much that I have to see to that my time is almost entirely taken up. But it won't be dull for her any longer now you have come. Ah, Evelyn, my love, you may say what you like—I know very well you *did* find it dull; it was only natural you should, and it's a great comfort to my mind to think it won't be so any longer. I shall be able to attend to everything properly without feeling uncomfortable about leaving you alone.'

And the good-natured gentlewoman proved perfectly content to act as a kind of superior housekeeper when her services were not needed as *chaperon*, so that, for the earlier part of the day, at all events, Evelyn and I were left to the undisturbed enjoyment of each other's society.

In spite of what I have previously said about my schooldays, I am not sure that those first few weeks at Tansted were not, after all, the most uninterruptedly happy period of my life. Evelyn grew dearer to me, and the sympathy and understanding between us more perfect with every hour we spent together. Even if I had never known her before, I could not have been so constantly with her without learning to love her now, and I was proud and glad to feel that she was as attached to me as I to her.

The days passed quietly and uneventfully enough, but they

never seemed long or monotonous. Evelyn was occupied with various charitable undertakings in the village, in which I rendered her what assistance I could; we took up some of our former studies again, and read and practised and sketched with a pleasant sense of our own virtue; there were delightful rides together, through leafy lanes and over wild heaths and commons, and long intimate talks, over old school memories, as we sat under the trees on the lawn of an afternoon, or paced the garden paths in the growing dusk.

My spirits recovered their tone in this wholesome, peaceful atmosphere. I should have been perfectly happy with Evelyn as my sole companion, but of course we could not remain in absolute seclusion, and my former morbid dislike to meeting people seemed to have almost disappeared, as I found, when I went with Evelyn to local gatherings, that I encountered none of the slights and coldnesses which had made me shrink from such ordeals in my own set at home.

All this I owed to Evelyn; she had made life seem fair and hopeful once more—and it would never be clouded again while she was with me, as, of course, she always would be now. Whether we lived on together all the years to come in this sweet old country home, or spent part of the time travelling abroad, was perfectly indifferent to me, so long as I had her by my side.

At times I fancied that she looked more fragile and delicate than when I first arrived, and seemed less and less inclined for exertion, but the excessive heat of that year's June was quite enough to account for it, and I felt no real uneasiness about her health, especially as she always declared she was perfectly well.

And, as it happened, when the day came which first shook my blind confidence in the future and revealed the Fool's Paradise in which I was living, the incident—if I may call so slight a thing an incident—that brought this about had nothing to do with the state of Evelyn's health.

It happened late one afternoon; we were to have gone to a garden-party at the Hall, but Evelyn had not felt equal to it at the last moment, and as I was not disposed to shelter myself under her aunt's too fluttering wing, I preferred to stay at home too, and leave Mrs Maitland to go alone and make our excuses.

We were still sitting on the lawn, though the first dinner-bell had rung, when the carriage returned with Mrs Maitland, who joined us with a little air of suppressed importance.

'Such a pleasant party, Evelyn,' she began; 'though almost too hot to move about. The Holliers were so disappointed not to see you—they sent the kindest messages. And really, I'm quite glad I went, for I've got a piece of news that I think you'll be pleased to hear. Whom *do* you think I met there? You'll never guess. That nice Mr Dallas we saw so much of at Florence. And just fancy, he has a place only a few miles from here—Laleham Court. Did you know that?'

'Mr Dallas!' exclaimed Evelyn, with more animation than she had shown all day. 'No, Aunt Lucy, I'd no idea of it. I never thought of him, somehow, as having any fixed home. How strange that you should have met him again like this.'

'My dear, we live in a small world after all,' said Mrs Maitland, with an evident sense of her own aphoristic originality, '*I* quite expected we should come across him again sooner or later. And he is most anxious to meet *you* again, my dear. I thought I might tell him that you would be charmed to see him, and he is going to ride over some afternoon soon. I *hope* I did right, Evelyn. You *will* be glad to see him, won't you?'

'Very,' said Evelyn, softly. 'I liked Mr Dallas. I hope he will come. I want you to meet him, Stella,' she added, turning to me. 'I know you have rather a contempt for young men in general, but I think you will admit that he is an exception.'

She spoke naturally enough, but there was a tender light in her eyes, a slight increase of colour in her cheeks that made my heart sink. Why was she so anxious to prejudice me in this man's favour? Why did she look at me in that wistful, almost pleading way, unless she wished to prepare me for something that might, that she hoped would, happen?

Evelyn went indoors shortly after, and Mrs Maitland and I were left together, when the suspicions I had already formed were more than confirmed.

'Has dear Evelyn ever happened to mention this Mr Dallas to you?' she asked. 'No? how very curious—I should have thought —but she is strangely reserved about some things. And really, I think she seemed pleased at the idea of meeting him, don't you? Strictly between ourselves, Miss Maberly, I have a strong impression—indeed, when we were at Florence I felt almost sure that on *both* sides—but though he was so much with us, there was hardly time for it to develop into— Still, now he is actually in the same neighbourhood, it *does* seem quite possible that—though of course it's too soon to speak as yet. It would be *such* a good thing. He's a great favourite of mine, most charming, and very well off. I hear Laleham Court is quite one of the show-places here. Everyone seems to think so much of him, too. *Exactly* the kind of man I should wish to see dearest Evelyn married to!'

These incoherent confidences were poured out on our way to the house, and I was soon able to escape to my room, and think over all they portended.

I felt almost stunned at first; it may seem strange, but the possibility of Evelyn's marrying some day had never struck me as anything but remote, since we had been associated.

I had suggested it that first afternoon while we were driving from the station, and she had repudiated any intention of marriage with a sincerity which would have reassured me subsequently had it occurred to me to feel any serious alarm.

But it did not, partly because Evelyn's nature seemed too spiritual somehow to be associated with earthly passion, partly because she had wound herself so closely round my heart that I instinctively shrank from the mere thought of losing her in such a way.

Now for the first time I had to face the fact that this was not only merely possible, but probable. I remember now that, even when she declared that she had decided never to marry, she had done so with a reservation to which her aunt had just given me the clue.

Evidently this Mr Dallas had made no ordinary impression upon Evelyn, though for some reason he had gone away without declaring himself; she had believed him indifferent, and that they were unlikely to meet again, but she had always had the faint hope that she might be mistaken, and this was the contingency which might make her reconsider her resolve to remain unmarried.

How I constructed all this out of so little I can hardly say, but I knew it as certainly as if she had told me so in words, and foresaw the almost inevitable future.

This man would appear sooner or later; the sight of Evelyn would revive his interest in her, if it had ever faded; their intimacy would be taken up again at the stage at which it had been interrupted, and, step by step, he would usurp my place in Evelyn's heart. I should have no right to complain; it would only be natural that she should put her lover before her friend. No doubt she would assure me that even marriage would make no difference in her affection for me, that, next to her husband, I should always be dearest in the world to her—but, even if this were true, it would not satisfy me. I could not be content now with any place but the first, and I already hated this unknown Prince Charming who was coming to thrust me into the background.

I felt a dull resentment against Evelyn, too, which was all the deeper because, at the bottom of my heart, I knew it was unreasonable. She might, I thought, have been more open with me; I had believed there were no secrets between us—and all the time she had kept this passage in her life to herself. I had a right to feel hurt and angry, but I would not let her see how sorely I was wounded; I would not condescend to a word of reproach, or any sign that I foresaw how speedily I should be abandoned. If she could be reserved, I would be still more so. And, besides, it was only prudent to steel my heart against her for the future, so as to be better able to bear to do without her when the time came, for if I was to be less than all in all to her, I was determined to be nothing.

So, from that evening, I began, almost insensibly, to alter in my manner towards Evelyn, and to put a certain distance between us. I said and did nothing which could give her any excuse to protest or ask for explanations; I kept up all the forms of our ordinary intercourse, but still, by slight, almost imperceptible, gradations, I withdrew from our former comradeship.

So sensitive a nature as hers could not help being affected by this, and I could see that she was vaguely uneasy and distressed by the consciousness of some unseen barrier between us, but I found a sombre satisfaction in the ingenuity with which I baffled all her advances, while still leaving her unable to determine precisely where or if she had been repelled.

It is strange how soon such a mental attitude as mine becomes rigid, until it is only to be relaxed by some extraordinary effort of will. I nursed my secret grievance against Evelyn until it was an absorbing and imperative necessity to find fresh food for it, and I was impatient for this friend of hers to appear and prove to me that my jealousy was only too well justified.

I had not to wait long. Mr Dallas rode over to call one afternoon that week, and I made my first acquaintance with the man who was to separate me from the only friend I had in the world.

As he came towards us across the lawn, my first impression was of a tall, well-built figure, a dark, smooth-shaven face, neither plain nor handsome, but with a look of undeniable distinction on it. When he glanced at me, as Evelyn introduced him, I saw that his eyes were grey, and calmly observant; he had an easy, quiet manner and a remarkably pleasant voice.

He made no secret of his pleasure at seeing Evelyn again, and she was equally frank in her welcome of him. They were soon deep in their Italian reminiscences, and as I was necessarily unable to take more than a listener's part in the conversation, I was the better able to watch them both; but whether my presence acted as a restraint upon them, or whether, as yet, they had not gone beyond the stage of friendship, I could detect nothing on his part or hers that absolutely bore out my suspicions.

He talked well, with an occasional touch of humour, and everything he said indicated considerable knowledge and culture, without a trace of priggishness or 'showing off.' He was certainly as different as possible from the rather heavy-witted young sportsmen whose conversation I had found so wearisome, and I could not help reluctantly admitting to myself that—dislike him as I might—there was something strangely attractive in his personality.

Occasionally courtesy obliged him to include me in the conversation, or explain some allusion for my benefit, but something —I did not know what—made me unusually tongue-tied and stupid that afternoon, and I was provoked to feel how unfavourably I must be impressing him.

Not that it mattered, of course. To him, if, indeed, he gave me a thought, I was merely the salaried companion, who was not expected to be brilliant or original. Why should I care about the opinion of a man to whom I was bound to be indifferent, and who was so evidently here for the sole sake of recommending himself to Evelyn?

She irritated me by the serenity with which she received all his attentions, as if she imagined I did not know how triumphant she felt at seeing him return to her, as if she could really be so insensible as she seemed to his personal charm.

It would have galled me even more, I daresay, if I could have surprised her in some self-betraying look or intonation, but my resentment against her had gained too strong a hold to make me care whether I was consistent or not, so long as I found fresh grievances to keep it alive.

He went away at last, and as I heard the sound of his horse's hoofs departing down the drive, the garden seemed to me to have grown dreary and deserted, and Mrs Maitland's chatter more unendurable than ever.

'Well, Stella?' said Evelyn, softly, looking at me with an expectant appeal in her eyes. I knew she wished to hear me praise this lover of hers, and I would rather have died just then.

'Well, Evelyn?' I returned.

'What do you think of him?'

'Of Mr Dallas? What *should* I think, except that he is the most irresistibly charming and accomplished and generally delightful person I ever met outside a novel?'

Her face clouded. 'If you talk in that ironical tone about him,' she said, 'I shall begin to think you dislike him—and yet I don't know why you should.'

'Why should you care whether I like him or dislike him, my dear?' I replied. 'What possible difference can it make to you—or to anyone else?'

I looked her in the face as I spoke, and saw that for the first time she hesitated and seemed confused.

'None, perhaps,' she said, 'and yet I shall be disappointed if you don't, Stella. But I believe you will, when you come to know him better.'

'I shall have plenty of time to study his many excellencies,' I said, 'if his visits are all as long as this one. I began to think he never *would* go.'

'I didn't think he stayed at *all* too long!' said Evelyn.

'Then, of course, my dear Evelyn, he didn't,' I retorted, as I rose; 'but all the same, he has contrived to give me a headache, and I must go indoors and lie down if I am to get rid of it by dinner-time.'

When I got upstairs I did not lie down, though my plea of a headache was not altogether a subterfuge. I paced the room, trying to realise what I actually felt towards this man. Why was it that the chief bitterness in my heart seemed concentrated upon Evelyn, when I had at least equal reason to hate him?

And suddenly the humiliating reason forced itself upon me, obstinately as I sought to keep it back.

I was no longer jealous of Hugh Dallas—I was jealous of Evelyn. And, as I realised all that this implied, I hid my burning face in my hands for very shame, though there was none to see.

III

Fool that I was, I had thought to do without Love, but he had found me out at last, and was punishing me for having set him at defiance. I had only met Hugh Dallas once, and yet I was already trying to recall his exact image, the tones of his voice, the least things I had heard him say; my heart was aching with the longing to see him again. My pride rebelled against it. I could not understand how this should have happened to me, how, in one short hour, the pivot of all my thoughts and hopes seemed to have shifted, or even what precise qualities he had which appealed to me so powerfully. Does one ever reason or analyse in such cases? I only knew that I loved him.

And he felt nothing but indifference towards me, probably had not noticed whether I was young or old, pretty or plain—how should he when all his thoughts were so evidently occupied with Evelyn?

I went to my mirror and studied myself curiously and dispassionately. I had certainly been looking my very best that afternoon. Surely the oval, olive-tinted face I saw reflected there, with the crown of soft dark hair, the imperious mouth, and the deep brown eyes that looked wistful and proud and sad, had a character and charm of its own which could bear comparison even with Evelyn's more fragile and spiritual loveliness. I was taller than she was; I was as shapely, as well-born; the cleverer in some respects. Why should I despair? He was not hers yet—was it so impossible that, if I chose, I might compel him, even now, to transfer his homage?

And yet I knew that I could not really sink to such baseness. After all, Evelyn had been good to me; I had loyalty and gratitude enough in me still to recognise that I would never repay her by robbing her of the love that was rightfully hers. But as I registered this vow I saw, with a bitter laugh at my own vanity, how ludicrously superfluous and cheap this magnanimity of mine was. For what had Evelyn to fear from me? She was everything to him already, and if she were not, she had the advantage of her wealth; it was not likely that Hugh Dallas would ever turn from the heiress to her penniless companion. How truly generous to renounce what I had not the remotest chance of ever possessing! No, such a love as mine was hopeless; the only course left to me was to preserve my self-respect in future by preventing him from ever suspecting my unhappy secret.

The surest way was to leave the home at once, and how often now I wish I had had the courage to do so. But I could not. What plausible excuse could I give Evelyn for leaving her so suddenly? She would guess my real reason. And I shrank from returning home and facing the astonishment and curiosity of my family— and where else was I to go?

I would stay at Tansted until I could remain no longer; I clung to the mere prospect of seeing him again. Anything was more bearable, even having to stand and look on at the rapid growth of his attachment to another, than going away and imagining it all. So I stayed on and hid the fox that was gnawing my heart, being sustained, as I then thought, by womanly pride, though I believe I was as much influenced by the old self-torturing impulse which led me to seek rather than shun the emotional excitement of misery.

Evelyn had no suspicion of my mad jealousy or the envy that jaundiced my every thought of her. As before, I took care to make any real confidence between us impossible, without allowing her to feel that I was estranged from her; she merely considered, as I knew she would, that I was suffering from a return of the old causeless depression that attacked me even in my school-girl days, and that it was wiser and kinder to leave me to fight it alone.

But the part I had resolved to play was more difficult and painful than I could have realised. Hugh Dallas became a more and more frequent visitor at Tansted; he had originally intended only to spend Whitsuntide at Laleham, but he stayed on, and seemed fully resigned to lose the remainder of the season in town. He had some idea, he said, of standing for his division at the next General Election, and it was necessary to cultivate his future constituents. How far he did this I could not tell, but he apparently found time to attend every social event at which there was any chance of Evelyn being present, and we were constantly meeting him at the various houses around Whinstone. At first he took some pains to be agreeable to me, as Evelyn's most intimate friend, and a person whom it was desirable to have on his side, but the mockery of this careless kindness was more than I could bear. I was afraid of betraying, in some unguarded moment, how deeply his presence agitated me, and I hid my feelings under a stony indifference, or cutting speeches at which my own heart bled while I was making them. I avoided him as much as I could, for it was better that he should believe I had an aversion for him than guess the truth.

I could see that he was hurt as well as surprised by my treatment, and that Evelyn, too, was distressed, and I felt a fierce satisfaction in knowing it; it was only fair that they should suffer a little when I was suffering so much.

She made tentative approaches to the subject when we were alone, but Evelyn was always easily repelled, and she soon saw that I did not intend to discuss it, and gave up the attempt with a sigh. The consciousness of the growing shadow between us was telling on her spirits, as I noticed, and every evidence of my supposed antipathy to Hugh Dallas was a fresh grief and anxiety to her.

I imagined that it was this which made her still hesitate before definitely accepting him, and that she did not love him enough as yet to brave my disapproval.

This impression of mine was strengthened by what I saw of their demeanour when they thought themselves alone and unobserved, for though I slipped away to my room at the first opportunity, I could not resist watching them whenever they were in the garden together and came within sight. They were always talking earnestly and confidentially; he, from his expression, seemed to be pressing her for a decision, and she gently putting him off without forbidding him all hope. Once or twice, as they passed below my window, I was almost certain I heard my own name.

I was the obstacle, I knew, but sooner or later he would succeed in persuading her to disregard my prejudices, though the suspense was so long drawn out that I almost fancied I should be glad when the comedy was over and the inevitable *dénouement* reached.

Even Mrs Maitland began to grow a little uneasy and impatient. 'I suppose it is really *all right*,' she said to me one afternoon, 'though *why* they should take so long to come to an understanding—I often feel tempted to try whether I can find out from dear Evelyn whether there is anything actually—but I might do more harm than good by interfering. Now *you*, dear Miss Maberly, you are naturally more in her confidence than I ever was—though I *am* her aunt. Don't you think that if you were to speak to her—?'

I gave the good lady to understand that I knew nothing and wished to know nothing, and that Evelyn was surely capable of managing her own affairs.

'I'm afraid you are getting to live far too much in a world of your own, my dear,' she retorted, with a slightly ruffled air. 'I thought you would take more interest in what concerns her happiness. But perhaps you don't feel at liberty to repeat confidences, and no doubt you are right, though I have *some* claim to be told, I consider, and you can certainly depend upon my discretion!'

She paused invitingly, but I saw no reason to gratify her curiosity, particularly as I knew no more than she did, and remained silent. 'Ah, well,' she continued, 'I certainly expected it would all have been settled *long* before this, but it's only a question of time after all. If she meant to refuse him she would not let him be so much with her as he is; she is far too conscientious for that.'

But as the time went on and nothing happened, I felt a growing dread of the day when the blow should fall. Even this uncertainty had its compensations—I could still indulge in faint delusive hopes. But when I knew that all was over, that they were definitely engaged, when I should have to witness their ecstasies, to sympathise, congratulate, when I found myself condemned to loneliness and dependence again, without even the excitement of occasional contact with him—how could I bear it, how could I live through it?'

And then the thought came to me: Why *should* I live through it? Why not escape from it all as soon as the misery became past all bearing?

They would not miss me at home; Evelyn might be a little sorry at first, but not for long. *He* would not care. And I should have done with suffering and be at rest.

I found a medical work in the library which treated of poisons, and this I studied carefully, for I had decided on this means of ending my life, and I wanted to find some drug that would act painlessly, and not leave me hideous after death. I chose chloral,[3] as the easiest to procure and the most likely to give the impression of an accidental overdose rather than deliberate suicide, so that I could go out of life carrying my secret with me.

It was not difficult to induce the chemist in the nearest market town to let me have enough for my purpose. I had dealt there before, and he was satisfied with entering my name and address, and mildly cautioning me against the danger of fighting insomnia (I told him I was suffering from sleeplessness), with so treacherous an ally.

So, now that I had the means at hand of procuring my own release whenever I chose, I felt calmer and more resigned.

One afternoon I was sitting in my room, absently wondering, as I fingered the fluted blue phial on my dressing-table, how long it would be before I broke the seal, and whether it was possible that I should repent as I felt the first approach of the sleep which would be my last, when I was startled by finding that Mrs Maitland had entered by the door, which I fancied I had locked.

'I'm afraid I disturbed you, my dear,' she began. 'But I knocked three times, and as you didn't answer, I ventured to peep in, for you have been so unlike yourself lately that I really feel quite anxious about you. . . . Why,' she broke off, as her eyes caught the phial, which I had not had presence of mind enough to hide in time, 'surely that bottle is labelled "poison." Now, what can you possibly want with such a thing?'

I laughed. 'Don't be alarmed,' I said, 'it's only a very ordinary sleeping draught. They're obliged to label it like this, but, as a matter-of-fact, it's perfectly harmless, so long as the proper dose is not exceeded. I got it because I've been afraid lately that I was in for a bad attack of neuralgia, and I thought I'd have a remedy at hand.'

'Neuralgia is a dreadful thing, I know,' she said, taking up the bottle and examining it. 'Ah, I see it tells you here how many drops to take—only I do hope you'll be very careful, my dear, and not take more than is safe—one hears of so many accidents.'

'If it will make your mind easier,' I said, 'I'll promise to take no more than is necessary, if I am ever reduced to taking it at all.'

'Thank you, my dear. So long as you keep to that and don't let yourself get *dependent* on it, I daresay—but I came up to tell you something, and I declare this has driven it quite out of my mind. Now, *was* it?'

I was naturally unable to supply the answer, and I daresay I looked as if I could see no reason why she should have invaded me at all in this unceremonious way.

'I remember now,' she said, 'of *course*—how stupid of me to forget! Mr Dallas is here again, and though, goodness knows, I was never an eavesdropper, I really couldn't help overhearing part of what he was saying to Evelyn just now, and from what I could make out, there *is* a hitch, and in some way it depends on you, my dear Miss Maberly, to put it right. It seems she has got it into her head that you disapprove of him—which, of course, is nonsense —and he was urging her to let him have an opportunity of seeing you, and I think she is willing to accept him if only he can succeed in getting you on his side—though why, as she is evidently fond of him, she should let *anyone* else—even *you*, my dear—dictate her answer to her, *I* don't know! But there it is, and though I'm sure that you see as well as I do myself what a thousand pities it would be if such a perfectly suitable match were broken off for some fanciful scruple, and I know you will make dear Evelyn understand how mistaken she is in thinking you could be opposed to anything so obviously for her happiness, I thought I had better give you just a hint how matters stand. And, now I've done it, I'll go away and not worry you any longer, for I see you're thinking me a tiresome old woman.'

She fussed out of the room, highly satisfied, I have no doubt, with her own consummate diplomacy, and I was left to think over what she had told me.

Part of it I had already guessed for myself, but it had never occurred to me that Evelyn would actually leave it to me of all people to decide what her answer should be. Such self-abnegation was unnatural, it could not be sincere; she had made up her mind to accept him long since, but she wanted to gain my formal approval to satisfy her own conscience, and she felt confident that I could not well refuse it.

And she had allowed *him* to plead to me—the man who would lacerate my heart by every word that showed how ardently he loved her! Could she really be so selfishly blind? After all, she was a woman; she ought to have—she *must* have read me better, in spite of myself, than to have no suspicion that it was not dislike which had made me shun him as I had. She had too much insight not to see, if she had cared to see, the cruelty of forcing me to figure like this in her triumph.

Still, I would go through this final ordeal; the fierce indignation I felt against both of them would give me strength to play my part to the end without faltering or betraying myself. He was there in the house now; if I chose to go downstairs I might get this interview over; I had never been alone with him yet. I felt a kind of eagerness for the exquisite suffering of hearing the avowal of his love for Evelyn from his own lips—death would be all the easier afterwards.

And so—though he would not notice whether I was looking ill or well—I hastily bathed my hot eyes and re-arranged my disordered hair, and feeling defiantly sure of myself, I went down to the drawing-room, where I knew he and Evelyn would probably be.

IV

As I expected, I found them together in the drawing-room, Hugh Dallas seated in the window-bay, and Evelyn at some distance from him. His troubled, despondent look was certainly not that of an accepted lover, and there was an air of constraint and consciousness in them both as I entered, from which I guessed that the conversation I had interrupted was chiefly about myself.

We talked for a while in a rather perfunctory manner, and I think that I was the most self-possessed of the three, and succeeded perfectly in hiding my torment of jealousy and suspense behind the mask of indifference that I had schooled myself to wear in his company. At last Evelyn made some pretext for quitting the room, and as she did so I saw the glance of secret encouragement she threw him.

We were alone together, he and I, for the first time since we had met, and I could hear the beating of my heart, even above the patter of the fountain on the lawn outside, in the silence. I watched him covertly as he sat there moodily pulling about some flowers in a vase which stood on the window-sill. I knew he was nerving himself to make an appeal to me. I knew, or thought I knew, what that appeal would be and suddenly I felt that I could not trust myself to listen to it. I had overrated my courage, and the one thing I desired now was to escape before the words were spoken. I had already risen with some incoherent excuse for joining Evelyn, when he stopped me with a mastery I felt powerless to defy.

'You will not go to Evelyn yet,' he said. 'I have something to say to you first, and you must hear it, Miss Maberly. Surely you will not refuse me so small a thing as that?'

There was a suppressed passion in his tone that thrilled me; for the moment I could almost have believed that it was I whose love he was seeking and even though I knew how cruelly fleeting such an illusion would prove, I surrendered myself to it.

'I will hear anything you wish to say to me,' I said.

'I want to know first,' he said, 'why you persist in looking upon me as an enemy?'

'Have I given you any reason for supposing so?' I asked. 'I don't think so.'

'Any reason?' he repeated. 'Have you ever condescended to be commonly civil to me? Would you speak to, or look at me? Would you be here in the same room with me, if you could help yourself? Do you suppose I am too dense to see that? Perhaps enemy is too strong a word; you may not think me sufficiently important to deserve even such a title as that, but you have taken very little trouble to hide the fact that you dislike me about as thoroughly as one human being can dislike another. You will not deny that?'

At least I had kept my wretched secret from him! It was some comfort even then.

'And if I do not deny it,' I said, 'what then?'

'I have the right to ask what I have done to deserve it—and I do ask.'

'I can give you no answer. Except that liking and disliking are sentiments beyond one's control.'

'Justice ought not to be at all events,' he retorted. 'Can you not be just to me? I don't claim to be a better sort of fellow than my neighbours, but I can honestly say that there is nothing in my life which makes me unworthy of any woman's friendship.'

Ah! I did not need to be told that—though he might have been the worst of men, and I should have loved him just the same. It was hard to see him standing there, pleading with me to lay aside what he supposed to be a rooted antipathy, and not to undeceive him by some mad words which would force him to understand my real feelings.

'Why should you wish to gain my friendship?' I said. 'It can make no difference to you whether you have it or not.'

'It makes this difference,' he said, 'that, unless I have it, I must keep away from Tansted for the future.'

'And you think Evelyn would be willing that you should go?' I said incredulously.

'She would be sorry, of course, but you must know that you have the first place in her heart. It distresses her too much to see, as she cannot help seeing, that my presence here is distasteful to you, that for some reason or other it has brought about a change in your feelings for her.'

'So she has sent you to me to try whether you cannot overcome my—my prejudices. Is that what I am to understand?'

'She thought that if I spoke to you and could get you to tell me plainly what you have against me, I might possibly succeed in showing you that you have judged me too harshly,' he replied. 'Look here, Miss Maberly, why can't you bring yourself to think of me as, at all events, a possible friend? Why do you wish to drive me away from Tansted altogether?'

'I shall not drive you away,' I said; 'it is I who will leave Tansted, and then you will be able to come here as before.'

'As if Evelyn or I would permit that. If you really detest me so much that, rather than endure the sight of me, you would separate yourself from such a friend as Evelyn, there is no more to be said. I must go away, give up all hope of happiness here. Is that what you wish? It rests with you.'

'It does *not* rest with me!' I said angrily. 'I will not have the responsibility thrust on me. And it is all so hollow and insincere. If Evelyn wishes to keep you she will—whether I approve or disapprove. It is a mockery to leave it to me like this.'

'I have already told you that Evelyn's first consideration is your happiness and peace of mind,' he said. 'I am bound to respect her feelings in the matter, to say nothing of yours. So I ask you once more whether I am to go or stay.'

'What is it to me which you do?' I cried wildly. 'Do I not know that, whatever I say, it will make no difference. Evelyn will be willing enough to make you happy when I am once out of the way. Why should you not marry when you are so plainly intended for one another? And I shall not care—do you understand that? I am utterly indifferent. Why should it matter to me, so long as I never see you again? There, I have given you your answer—now let me go.'

'Yes, I have had my answer,' he said. 'I hoped it would have been a kinder one; but I suppose I had no right to expect anything

else from you. Our interview,' he added grimly, as he held open
the door for me, 'has not been such a pleasant one that I should
wish to prolong it. Good-bye, Miss Maberly, you need not be
afraid of any further persecution from me. You have shown me
plainly enough that your decision is final.'

I passed out without venturing to look at him, and went up to
my own room. I felt relieved, elated, at having triumphed over
my own weakness. I had met him face to face and without faltering; he would never suspect now my real feelings towards him.
I could almost believe that I really *had* ceased to care—or how
came it that my suicidal intentions of an hour or so ago seemed
only cowardly and sentimental.

I had courage to go on living now, if only to see how Evelyn
would act when she found that I could not be cajoled into sanc-
tioning her desertion of me, and how long it would be before her
pretended scruples were thrown to the winds.

We did not meet again till dinner, when, although we were
obliged to keep up some sort of conversation on indifferent
topics, I could tell by her troubled expression that Hugh Dallas
had informed her before leaving of the result of his appeal.

I evaded our usual after-dinner stroll in the garden by pleading
that I had a headache and wished to be quiet, so she and Mrs Maitland went without me. I sat in the drawing-room, in the same
seat in which I had listened to *him*, and tried to imagine him there
in the window-bay, and to live through the scene again, sentence
by sentence. The butler brought in the lamps without disturbing my reverie, and the trees outside were becoming a blurred
bronze against the violet evening sky, before I heard Evelyn enter
the room softly.

'Is your head better now, Stella?' she said, coming up to me and
laying one hand on my shoulder, 'because—if you will let me—I
want to talk to you about—about somebody.'

I shrank involuntarily from her light touch. 'I know what you
want to say,' I said, 'and it will be no good—you will only waste
your words!'

'But you will hear me, dearest,' she said. 'We have been such
friends till—till something came between us. Don't harden yourself against me now. You must know how I love you! Stella, you

sent Hugh away this afternoon very unhappy. It makes *me* miserable, too, to find that you are so bitterly prejudiced against him. I like him very dearly. *Can't* you try to like him a little, for my sake? It will grieve me to have to send him away, but, if you really cannot bring yourself to tolerate him, what else can I do?'

'Why do you insist on making *me* responsible?' I said. 'Except to put me in the wrong! I tell you I will have nothing to do with it. You are your own mistress—do as you choose.'

'How can I choose to make you wretched and uncomfortable, Stella! This is your home as well as mine, and as long as you and I are together I want you to be happy here, as you were at first. And though I was afraid to say anything, I have fancied lately that you are not happy with me. Was I right?'

'I never *am* happy long anywhere,' I said impatiently. 'I get unsettled and restless. And I—I don't think this place agrees with me quite. I shall have to leave you sooner or later, Evelyn; it had better be soon.'

'Leave me, Stella!' she exclaimed. 'I hoped that nothing would ever separate you and me!'

Did she actually imagine that I could live in the same house —with them?

'Not even Hugh Dallas?' I said sardonically.

'Laleham is not so far from here—we should not be separated, even then. But you say you dislike him so. I begin to wonder, Stella, whether you are not the least bit jealous?

I felt myself turning hot. 'Jealous,' I cried. 'What do you mean, Evelyn—do you suppose—?'

'Don't be jealous any more, dear, there is no need. I *do* like him very much, he is so manly and honourable. I feel sure that he will make the woman he loves very happy, Stella, but still—but still, he can never be what *you* are to me, and if you tell me that you really cannot—'

'I hate insincere talk like that, Evelyn,' I interrupted. 'You don't mean it—and you know you don't.'

She flushed painfully. 'You are very strange to-night, Stella,' she said. 'I don't know why you should think I am not sincere. But I would rather see the two dearest friends I have liking and respecting one another, and I do want you to make an effort to overcome this antipathy so that we could all three be happy. After all, you can have no *real* reason for it. You have got some morbid, fanciful idea into your head about him, which I know I could convince you in a moment was unjust. Trust me, Stella. Tell me you dislike him.'

'I will not be catechised like this,' I said, writhing in impotent anger; 'it is too humiliating! You are simply trying to exasperate me. You *do* understand, or if you really don't, you might have before this—only you were too blinded by your own selfishness!'

'Am I selfish? and blind, too?' she said slowly. 'Tell me how, Stella; it is the least you can do.'

'Very well, I *will* tell you, though you know it already. You are not a fool, Evelyn, and even a fool might have guessed that if I avoided him and made him believe I detested the very sight of him, it was because—because I was afraid of myself. . . . Do you want me to go on?'

'Stella!' she exclaimed. 'Oh, you were right. I *have* been blind. If you had only confided in me.'

'I had some pride left,' I retorted. 'I would have kept it from every living soul if I could, and now you have succeeded in wringing it out of me. Be satisfied with that, and leave me in peace.'

'You don't understand,' she cried. 'It is so sudden and bewildering that I—but I shall be able to tell you in a moment how—'

'The less we say now the better it will be for us both,' I said. 'You see now what a mockery the word friendship is between us, and how necessary it is that we should part.'

'We need not,' she cried. 'Stella, did I not tell you all I cared for was your happiness? Well—'

'For heaven's sake, don't go through the farce of offering to give him up!' I said scornfully. 'As if he would be likely to allow himself—as if I would *accept*. I will listen to no more of this hypocritical cant . . . See, I have stopped my ears. Say what you please now—I shall hear nothing!'

She caught my hands in hers and drew them down. 'You *shall* hear me, you foolish, wilful girl,' she said. 'I won't *let* you wreck your own life like this!'

I wrenched myself free with such violence that she staggered back and fell into a couch, on which she lay, white and panting, looking up at me as I stood over her in a tempest of ungovernable fury.

'Be silent, do you hear,' I said. 'I warn you that, if you say a single word more just now, I can't answer for what I may do. I might *kill* you! If you are wise, go away, and leave me to myself —go away!'

She rose to her feet unsteadily, her eyes misted over with pain and apprehension and appeal as they met mine; she drew a long gasping sigh and pressed her hand to her left side, and then, supporting herself on her way by chairs and couches, she slowly went out of the room, leaving me standing there, already a little ashamed of my outburst, but sullen and impenitent still. Everything was at an end between us; meek and spiritless as she was, she must recognise that we could never be the same to one another again, that my confession had made a chasm that nothing could ever bridge. It was a relief to have delivered my soul, to have done with all dissimulation, and yet I cursed my insane folly in allowing the one thing I was bound to conceal to be extorted from me, and I hated Evelyn for having driven me beyond prudence.

She had been so irreproachably correct throughout, so maddeningly forbearing and gentle, she had put me so hopelessly in the wrong—and now I was at the mercy of her discretion, and some day or other she would infallibly confide my secret to him —and he would despise and pity me. At least I would not be there to see it. I would leave Tansted the very next day, even if—which was not likely—Evelyn tried to keep me—any place was better than this now. How long I sat nursing these bitter and angry thoughts, I don't know; it was late, and the servants had locked up and gone to bed, before I heard footsteps descending the stairs and entering the room. Could it be Evelyn coming to patch up a peace? I would have none of her forgiveness, she should know how I hated her, and how determined I was that this should be the last night I ever spent under her roof.

But the footsteps were not light enough for Evelyn's. When I turned, it was to see Mrs Maitland in a loose wrapper,[4] with a look of severity and decision that was unusual on her flaccid, good-natured countenance. 'I came down, Miss Maberly,' she said, 'to ask you to tell me what is wrong with Evelyn. I can get nothing from her—and you can probably enlighten me if you choose. Has she made up her mind to refuse Mr Dallas, or has she not? If she has, and you have induced her to do it, may Heaven forgive you!'

'I know no more about her intentions than you do,' I replied haughtily. 'If she refuses Mr Dallas it will not be through any inducements of mine—and it is useless to demand explanations from me in that very peremptory tone.'

She changed her manner at once. '*Was* I peremptory, my dear? I'm sure I didn't intend to be, and I beg your pardon. But I am so worried and uneasy about it, and I thought perhaps you — The poor dear child is dreadfully distressed about *something*. I was quite shocked when I went in to see how ill she was looking, and I'm sure she had been crying. She has been trying to write a letter to Hugh Dallas, I'm afraid, and she is really unfit for it just now.'

Writing to him! Writing to tell him—of course from the highest and most unselfish motives—what she had just wormed out of me, to propose that impossible renunciation to him— Could the most feline malice invent a more crushing and humiliating revenge?

'Trying to write,' I repeated; 'then she has not written yet?'

'I think she had made one or two attempts and torn them up.'

'Don't let her write to-night,' I said. 'Persuade her to give it up and go to bed.'

'My dear, I tried—but she declares she can't sleep until she has written. I wonder,' she added, 'whether if I gave her just a few drops of that sleeping draught you have—'

'Do,' I said eagerly. 'You will find it on my table; make her take some at once.'

'You are sure it is quite safe?'

'Yes, yes, perfectly. It can do her no harm. The dose is on the label and she ought to get to sleep at once, and not think about that letter till morning.'

'She will be really ill to-morrow unless she can have a good night's rest, and I've no bromide or sulphonal[5] or anything. I really think I had better— On your table, you said? Then, goodnight, my dear, and don't sit up too late yourself, for I'm sure *you* look as if you needed sleep too.'

She left me to myself, and for the first time I was thankful for her fussiness, for her suggestion of the sleeping-draught would effectually prevent that letter from being written that night. To-morrow I would see Evelyn and compel her, by every argument I could think of, to abandon her quixotic intention.

If she could only be induced to take the draught at once. I wanted to be sure. I felt stifled indoors; outside there would be air, and I might find out what I was so anxious to know. It was easy to slip back a bolt or two on the hall door, and soon I was outside in the warm darkness.

From the lawn I could see Evelyn's window. The curtains were drawn, but above them a slender bar of light told me that she was still up. Perhaps the letter was now being written that would present her to him as more angelic and adorable than ever; and render me odious and despicable in his eyes. Oh, how intensely I hated her at that moment. Whether she believed herself sincere, or whether she was the most consummate of hypocrites, she was equally betraying my secret, exposing me to the ignominy of being refused by the man to whom I had given my heart unasked.

Was it then, as I stood there under the cedar, that it flashed across my mind that in the medical book I had consulted I had read a statement that chloral, even in the smallest doses, was extremely dangerous in any case of weakness of the heart?

And had not Evelyn, that first afternoon as we were driving from the station together, told me that once, at all events, her heart had been considered to be affected?

I have tried and tried in vain to be quite clear when this first occurred to me. There are even times when I have terrible doubts whether both these facts may not have been present to my mind from the very first—even when Mrs Maitland was suggesting chloral. I cling to the hope that, bitter as my feelings were towards Evelyn, I was guiltless, even in thought, of such wickedness as that. I cannot believe that I was really capable of wilfully allowing her to encounter any peril which I could have prevented. I have enough to reproach myself with, God knows, without that!

No, it was not till later, I am sure of that, not till the moment when, as I stood watching, I saw the bar of light suddenly die out.

And then, as soon as I realised the danger, my first impulse was to rush up, arouse Mrs Maitland, find out whether the drug had been taken as yet, and what could be done.

But if Evelyn had already taken the chloral it would be too late to interfere. She might not have needed it at all. In any case, was it certain that it would do her the slightest harm? People outgrew weakness of the heart; she was no longer an invalid—perhaps she had never even had anything really wrong with her heart; young girls often like to fancy they are suffering from some interesting malady; doctors can make mistakes.

And if I alarmed Mrs Maitland by my misgivings, what would she think? Why, that I had really been contemplating Evelyn's death, and was seized with tardy remorse! I should be exposing myself to the most dreadful suspicions—all for a risk which most likely only existed in my over-excited imagination.

I argued all this with myself over and over again as I walked the lawn feverishly, backwards and forwards, unable to arrive at any conclusion for long, until at last, too exhausted bodily and mentally to go on thinking, I sank into one of the wicker seats that had been left in the garden. Why torment myself any longer when no action was possible? It was out of my hands now; and, besides—nothing *would* happen.

And then I was so worn out by all I had gone through since that afternoon that I suppose I must have fallen asleep in the chair, for I was not conscious of anything more until I was roused by a sense of chillness in the air, and opened my eyes to see the eaves and gables of the old house before me looking unnaturally sharp and distinct in the livid light of approaching daybreak, and the sky above already starless and mottled with pearl and opal clouds. I rose shivering and went indoors, still overcome with drowsiness, and, once in my room, threw myself on my bed without undressing, in the hope that sleep would come when I closed my eyes. But I only succeeded in dozing for a few minutes at a time, and soon the daylight that filtered in through my blinds, and the first feeble cheeping of the birds outside, made even this impossible, and I lay there, trying wearily to identify the various objects in the room, and strangely baffled and irritated by being unable to account for a grey square on my table that seemed unfamiliar.

As the light increased it revealed the square as a letter, and with an irrational hope of finding it a note from Mrs Maitland to tell me that she had not given Evelyn the chloral, I sprang up and drew the curtains in order to read it. Then my mind would be set at rest, and I could sleep.

But when I tore the envelope open it was Evelyn's handwriting that I saw, and though it is long since I last had that letter in my hands, I believe I can remember it almost word for word, as I read it then:

'I have begun this several times,' she wrote, 'and torn it up, and yet I can't sleep until I have put an end to all this misunderstanding. I know so well that you will be even more wretched than I am, you poor, self-tormenting Stella! I would have told you—but you were not yourself, you would not have listened, and I was afraid of driving you into saying or doing something you would regret if I tried any more just then.

'But now I have a superstitious feeling that, if I don't tell you at once, this very night, something that will change all your thoughts of me, you may never know, and so, perhaps, miss a great happinesss.

'Hugh is nothing to me, Stella, has never been anything but a very dear friend. Perhaps, at one time, at Florence, he might —but I felt that my hold on life was so slight then that I had no right to let him care for me in that way. And since then—where were your eyes, Stella, that you could not see how devotedly he has come to worship you? though he almost despaired of ever touching your heart. You were so proud, so resolute in keeping him at a distance, that you misled us both. I quite believed that you had taken one of your obstinate dislikes to him, and that his only chance was in time and patience. We had long and anxious consultations over it, and I could only promise that I would do my best for him, when all the time—! If you had only let me talk to you about him, only shown the slightest sign of interest, I would have told you how it was my dearest wish, ever since I first heard he was a neighbour of ours, that you and he might make each other happy.

'But I know now—and I understand that you were silent out of loyalty to me, and love and admire you all the more for it, and I mean to make you happy in spite of your wilful, obstinate self, for I made him promise to come over to-morrow as usual, in case I could induce you to relent. I can tell him now—though you may be sure that I shall not say a word you would not wish me to say —but I can let him understand that you feel you have been too hasty, and that he need not give up all hope just yet.

'As for you and me, Stella, let us forget that this cloud has ever come between us; we will never speak of it, never think of it again, unless to rejoice that it has passed and left our love all the firmer.

'There is so much I want to say—but I am too tired to sit up any longer, and I feel I shall sleep soundly now. I shall tell Saunders to put this on your dressing-table, so that you will see it before you go to bed, and now good-night, Stella, love me always, and never never have bad thoughts about me again.'

Not even my hard and embittered heart could be proof against the love and generosity and delicacy which spoke in every sentence of this letter and overwhelmed me with shame and contrition. Was there ever such perversity of misconstruction, such readiness to impute my own base thoughts to others, such ingenuity in making myself and them miserable, as I had been guilty of all these wretched weeks?

What could I ever say and do to show Evelyn how sincerely I repented? That, though she had forgiven me, I could never entirely forgive myself? How long would it be before I could go to her room and pour out all my penitence and gratitude? How impatiently I realised that it was too early as yet, that I must not venture to disturb her slumber for several hours to come.

And after the first sharpness of shame and remorse I began to feel the exquisite thrill of a joy that would not be quite suppressed; in vain I tried to think only of my wickedness and folly. My heart would throb wildly with the knowledge that Hugh Dallas loved me, all unlovable as I was, that an immense, unhoped-for happiness was coming to me with the brightness of the summer morning, and the expanding flowers, and the triumphant trilling and piping of birds.

At last I could resist the impulse to go to Evelyn no longer; if she was asleep, I would sit beside her and wait until she awoke—I might find her awake already.

I went to her door and opened it softly; the curtains were thick and shut out the light so effectually that all was grey and indistinct at first, but I could see that Evelyn was still asleep, lying with her face turned from me and her right hand extended, palm upwards, as if seeking to be clasped. I laid mine upon it—was it my fancy that made it seem so strangely chill and unresponsive? And why could not my ear detect any sound of breathing? I recollected the chloral; no doubt that would have produced a deeper sleep than usual—I was giving way to fanciful terrors again; when I had let in the light, the reassuring, everyday light, I should see that all was well.

I drew the curtains—softly, for fear of waking her; the light poured in, and the cool air of morning met my cheeks through the open casement. Thrushes were hopping about the turf, and the sky between the cedar branches was tinged with saffron and rose.

And I turned and saw Evelyn's face and realised the cruel and awful truth. Nothing would wake her any more, no words of love and sorrow would ever reach her. She was dead.

V

I think that even those who have felt least sympathy with me hitherto will find some pity for me now in the first terrible shock of my discovery that Evelyn was dead.

I refused to believe it at first, in spite of appearances. I tried every restorative, every test I could think of—and all was in vain, until in my despair I felt something like anger with the form that lay there, so still and passive, with the lips parted in a half smile that seemed a tender mockery of my efforts.

She was dead, and I might rouse the house and send for doctors, but nothing would make any difference—they would only tell me what I knew already. I recognised at last how useless it was to seek any longer for signs of the life that had fled, and I stood there in a dazed stupor, repeating to myself, over and over again, 'Evelyn is dead. She will never know now how bitterly I repent, how dearly I love her. I shall never hear her speak to me again. She is dead—quite dead—' until the words lost their meaning.

If only, even now, I could wake to find it all a ghastly dream —but no, I knew it was too hideously real, the horrible irony of having been so near happiness and missing it thus, the thought of all that hung upon Evelyn's life, the part she was to have taken in bringing Hugh Dallas and me together, and the impassable gulf her death had set between us—all this came upon me with crushing force, and I fell on my knees, writhing, in speechless, tearless agony, by the bed where she lay unheeding—and out in the garden the pitiless birds sang louder and merrier every moment.

I knew I ought to take some action, call someone, not to leave the household any longer in ignorance of what had happened, but I could not stir. I would wait a little longer still; there might —who knew?—there might be a miracle wrought, if I prayed, if I wrestled hard enough with Heaven to give me back my dead. God had heard such prayers before; would He be more cruel to me when my need was as great as—nay, greater far than that of those others? Surely He would see that my punishment was heavier already than I could bear.

And I prayed—unceasingly, frantically, seeking by passionate entreaties, arguments, promises, to move that far-off Tribunal to set back its decrees, just this once more, and allow this one soul to return through the gates that had scarcely closed as yet. Was not all possible to an omnipotent and merciful God?

Thus I entreated and implored—but there was no answering sign. God saw my misery and heeded it not; it was useless to appeal any longer, since He was either indifferent or powerless, and then in my reckless raving I besought whatever power there might be—good or evil, angel or devil, on earth or in hell—that heard me, to come to my aid now in my desperate extremity, and make that which was dead alive.

But hardly had the impious words left my lips than I was appalled at my blasphemy, and implored that my Creator would pardon me for even momentarily doubting His omnipotence, and show me of His infinite mercy and goodness—even now, little as I deserved it.

And, while I still knelt, the sun rose and shot a level ray of crimson gold into the room, suffusing Evelyn's pale, pure face with the hue of life and health, until, as I looked, the illusion was so powerful that I buried my face in the bedclothes lest I might be cheated into hope.

For I knew then, as I had known all the time, that I was asking the impossible; the age of miracles was past—the dead return to us no more. I must try to bear my load of grief and remorse with patience, until Heaven saw fit to let us meet again, and all would be understood and forgiven.

But suddenly I became aware of a slight stir beneath the coverlet, a sound like the faintest sigh. I raised my head, hardly daring to hope that my senses had not duped me afresh—and then, with a relief so acute and overpowering that it was almost agonising, and a mental shock that numbed my brain for the moment, I saw Evelyn's breast heave and her eyelids quiver and her eyes light up with the life that a moment before seemed to have died out of them for ever!

I caught her slight, unresisting form in my arms and kissed the sweet, wondering face, calling her by the maddest, fondest names, laughing and weeping, beside myself with the unspeakable joy of finding her warm and living, who but just now had lain there dead and cold.

She submitted to my caresses without returning them, seeming but half awake, a strange wonder still lingered in her eyes, as though they had looked upon the secrets of the life beyond and could not forget them all at once; her very smile was charged with mystery.

'Where am I?' she said dreamily. 'How do I come to be here, and who are you?'

'Evelyn!' I cried; 'don't you know me? I am Stella—Stella Maberly. Say that you are beginning to remember—that you forgive me for all I said and did last night!'

'Last night!' she repeated vaguely. 'Tell me, Stella, for I seem to have forgotten.'

Brokenly and incoherently I poured out my confession, keeping back nothing, exaggerating rather than extenuating all my harsh words and evil thoughts. I told her of the chloral; I accused myself of being her murderess in all but deed. I described how I had read her letter, and come in—to find her lying there, to all appearances dead.

She covered her eyes with her slender hands for a minute or so, as if to reflect and remember, and then she looked at me, still with that questioning scrutiny. 'I do begin to recollect now,' she said slowly. 'What a fright you must have had, Stella. But what has become of the chloral? Oh, I see—you had presence of mind enough to get rid of it as soon as you saw what had happened. That was prudent!'

The phial was certainly gone, as I noticed now for the first time.

'Evelyn!' I cried, sorely hurt. 'You can't really suppose I could think of any danger to myself *then!* As if anything could matter but that I had lost you. I could only pray—and God heard me. He has let you come back to me, oh, my dear! my dear! He has let you come back!'

She let her hands lie passively in mine, and lay smiling, with a soft gleam under her half-shut eyelids.

'He has let me come back,' she said. 'How good of Him! How grateful you must be—and what much greater care you will take of me for the future, will you not, Stella?'

There was something in her tone which was not exactly flippancy or mockery, but rather a touch of delicate irony, which, however playful and affectionate, jarred on me at such a moment. Irony of any sort was so unlike Evelyn. But how could I give such a trifle more than a passing thought in the rapture I felt at having her back alive and well? I could only again protest my shame for having misjudged her, my willingness to be her devoted friend, her servant, her slave, anything she would permit me to be—in future, and beg her for some assurance that I had not quite lost her confidence and affection, in spite of all my unworthiness.

'You must give me time, Stella,' she said languidly. 'I don't

understand it all yet—there is a great deal that I have to get accustomed to; everything seems strange, even this place, as if I had
been away a long long time. I want to be alone and think.'

I could readily understand that the effect of the opiate had not
quite worn off as yet, and that she must have been shocked, and
bewildered, too, by my overstrung and hysterical confessions, so
I left her to recover full possession of her faculties in peace.

It was still early, but I was too excited and happy to sleep. I had
my bath, dressed and went down to the garden, to taste the full
sweetness of the contrast between my present bliss and my condition when I last paced those paths in miserable uncertainty and
dread a few short hours ago.

Standing there in the fresh morning air, watching the first
spiral of smoke ascend from the old chimney-stacks into the
golden-blue sky, and hearing the cheerful sounds of awakening
life from the offices and stables, it was impossible to retain the
idea of any supernatural element in Evelyn's recovery of animation. I could see now that no miracle had happened; the drug had
thrown her into a sleep so profound that it had the appearance
of death, and my conscious-stricken imagination had led me to
believe the worst. But, whether I had cause or not for gratitude, I
did feel deeply thankful to Heaven when I thought of the anguish
and desolation which this day had seemed so certain to bring, and
which I had been spared.

And soon even this was forgotten in the recollection of what
Evelyn had told me of Hugh Dallas. I should see him so soon—
this very afternoon, perhaps, and she would have reassured him,
he would understand at least that there was hope for him if he
still cared to persevere. And if he did care—as I knew he would—I
should act the woman's delicious comedy of seeming gradually
to soften towards the man she secretly adores, here, in this dear
old garden-world, through the golden hours that were coming
to me.

A new radiance was on the familiar landscape. Everything I
saw around me had become strange and wondrous and beautiful;
the ripple of light and shade over the distant cornfields, the long
violet shadows cast by the trees on the dew-silvered pasture land,
the colour and fragrance of the flowers, the flitting of yellow but-

terflies about the lawn, every common thing, in short, filled me
with a keenness of delight that was like an additional sense.

This state of rapturous ecstasy made me lose all count of time,
and I was startled to find that I had been roaming about for hours,
and that the gong was sounding for breakfast.

Neither Evelyn nor her aunt had come down as yet, and, as
I waited for them, I wondered how I had never before appreci-
ated the charm of the long, low-ceilinged morning-room with
its panelled walls and stately old furniture; the sun had not as yet
struck further in than the faded crimson of the window cushions,
though it shone in full glare upon the conservatory at the further
end, where the masses of bloom and transparent green foliage
made a vivid contrast to the cool, subdued light of the room
itself. The very breakfast-table, with its dainty china and gleaming silver, heightened the luxurious sense of well-being and the
delightfulness of mere existence, which made the world seem so
good to live in that morning.

And yet, when Evelyn appeared, as she did presently with Mrs
Maitland, I felt, almost from the moment she entered, as if my
exhilaration had received an unaccountable check.

Why, I could not understand; she was looking brighter and
fresher than she had done for weeks. She greeted me with a
gaiety and good-humour that seemed to ignore all that had happened—and yet I could not resist an uneasy fancy that in some
way her attitude to me had changed, that my impulsive confession had killed for ever the guileless trust and affection she had
given me before.

After we had sat down to breakfast and the butler had left the
room, she said: 'Aunt Lucy has been paying me the most extravagant compliments on my appearance, Stella, I hope *you* see an
improvement in me too?'

'You are looking wonderfully well, dear Evelyn,' I said. 'Better
than I could have hoped.'

'Hoped—when?' she said; 'last night—or early this morning?'

I could not answer. The tone in which she asked the question,
rather than the question itself, sent a chill to my heart. I could
not have believed that she would treat so lightly what had passed
between us.

'Stella came into my room this morning, Aunt Lucy, and found me so sound asleep that she fancied I was never going to wake again,' she explained.

'Indeed, my dear, you were only half awake when I came in to see you just now,' said her aunt, 'for you didn't know me in the least. I assure you, Miss Maberly, I positively had to tell her who I was.'

'Wasn't it stupid of me?' said Evelyn. 'And I frightened poor Stella so that she said the wildest things. She was quite persuaded that she had killed me—why, is more than I quite understand, even now. What made you imagine yourself so guilty, Stella?'

I looked at her appealingly; her eyes met mine with a malicious challenge in them which I knew I could not avoid by silence. 'I told you,' I said, in a voice I could not steady,—'I told you that I thought the chloral—' I could not finish the sentence, the recollection of all the agony of those minutes overpowered me.

'Ah, the chloral—I remember now,' she said. 'Aunt Lucy tells me she took it away last night, and it will be a great relief to me, Stella, if you will let it remain in her keeping. It is such a danger-ous drug that I do trust you will have nothing to do with it in future—one so easily makes mistakes.'

I could not trust myself to reply. I knew too well that all these speeches, though worded so as to convey nothing of their real significance to any ear but mine, were so many deliberate taunts. Why did she take this cat-like pleasure in torturing me—she, who had never before uttered a cruel word? Any other sign of estrangement I could have understood—but this was too utterly foreign to all my conceptions of her.

Mrs Maitland saw, I think, that the subject was distressing to me, and with her usual good-nature, turned it off by remarking how delighted she was to see that Evelyn had at last recovered her appetite. I had already noticed that Evelyn was eating more heartily than I ever remembered to have seen her, and with a daintily sensuous enjoyment, which somehow made her seem more charming.

'I'm ravenous this morning,' she said. 'I feel as if I had eaten nothing for ages. You must try not to feel horrified, both of you.'

'My dear,' replied her aunt, 'I'm sure we are both only too pleased to see such a change. I really think this country life has begun to do you good at last. You have certainly come down quite a different creature this morning.'

'A different creature,' she repeated with a gay little laugh; 'is that *your* opinion of me, Stella? You are bound to put up with me at all events, are you not, whatever I am.'

When breakfast was over, and she and I were in the room alone together, she wound her arm round me and drew me up to an old-fashioned mirror in a tortoiseshell frame that hung on one of the walls. 'Come and help me to make the acquaintance of my new self,' she said. 'I want to know whether you approve of me. Really, I think you ought to feel satisfied, *I* do.'

As I stood there and saw our two faces reflected side by side, I thought that surely Evelyn had never looked so lovely before, her cheeks had never worn so vivid a rose, her eyes had never shone with that starry radiance, her smile had never been so dazzling —and yet, even while I felt her arm pressing me closer to her, I could not prevent a shiver of apprehension, a growing distrust and dread which I knew to be unreasonable.

She noticed the pallor and trouble in my face, the uncontrollable shrinking under her embrace.

'Why, Stella,' she said, in a tone between amusement and concern, 'you are trembling! Is it possible that you can be afraid— of me?'

'I—I don't know,' I faltered. 'I don't think I am afraid—I don't want to be!'

'Up there—in that room—you promised to love me more devotedly than ever,' she said softly. 'Is this how you begin?'

'You won't let me,' I cried. 'You have not forgiven me. If you had, you would not delight in reminding me of what you know must give me pain, of what I would willingly forget. You don't look at me as if you loved me—and it frightens me, Evelyn. There is a change in you, and I see it!'

She shrugged her shoulders. 'Naturally, there is a change —after what has happened,' she said. 'But, think—would you rather that your beloved Evelyn was lying, white and cold and silent for ever, upstairs at this moment than have me here by your side? What is done cannot be undone—and it will be wiser of you to accept me as I am.'

'You can't believe that I am anything but unspeakably glad and grateful that you are spared to me—whether you love me or not!' I cried passionately. 'Say, at least—at least—that you don't doubt *that!*'

'I do not doubt it,' she replied. 'You have too much reason to be both, my dear. Only, I expect to be given proofs of your sincerity—that is all. There, don't distress yourself any more about it. I have no ill-feeling whatever towards you—why should I?'

She kissed me with a kind of careless, half-contemptuous clemency as she spoke, but I could not feel consoled or reassured. It was too plain that the sudden discovery of my baseness had, for the time, shaken her faith in friendship, and driven her into cynical disbelief in any disinterested affection. I had tried her too far, and done harm that it would be long before I could entirely repair, if it ever could be entirely repaired.

It was my punishment, and I must accept it, since I had deserved a far heavier penalty even than the forfeiture of Evelyn's confidence. I might have lost *her*.

A little later we were in the garden when Mrs Maitland came out. 'I only wanted to know, dear Evelyn,' she said, 'before I saw the cook, whether it is at all likely that Mr Dallas may dine with us this evening; that is, if he *is* coming over this afternoon?' There was an irrepressible curiosity in her eyes as she looked at Evelyn, which showed that her question was not wholly prompted by household considerations.

'Mr Dallas?' said Evelyn, with apparent unconcern. 'Is he coming over? Very likely he may. You had better ask Stella, had you not?'

'Nonsense, my dear!' said Mrs Maitland, with some irritation, 'it is a question for you and nobody else, and really I think it is time you took me a little more into your confidence, and I must have a little private talk with you on the subject. I am sure Miss Maberly will excuse us.'

She drew Evelyn away, and I heard no more, but I could see them walking up and down the paths in the fruit garden, Evelyn bending her graceful head in demure attention, or occasionally stopping to strip off a bunch of currants as she passed, and Mrs Maitland talking earnestly and emphatically.

Presently Evelyn returned alone, and threw herself into a chair by my side.

'Have you told her?' I asked impulsively.

'I think my invaluable Aunt Lucy monopolised the conversation,' said Evelyn, smiling, more to herself than to me. 'She was most informing. Have I told her what, Stella?'

'Ah, you *know!*' I exclaimed. 'And—and don't you see that Mrs Maitland believes that Hugh—Mr Dallas, is in love with *you?*'

'She made no secret of it,' said Evelyn. 'And if he is, my dear, what then?'

'Can you ask? After the letter you wrote me—only last night? You cannot have forgotten!'

'Absolutely—my mind is a perfect blank on the subject. I gather from you that you and I quarrelled last night rather seriously. Was it about this Hugh Dallas, by any chance?'

'You only pretend to be ignorant to punish me. You *must* remember!'

'All that happened before this morning, my dear Stella. I can remember nothing until I am reminded. Show me this letter, and no doubt it will enlighten me.'

It was not altogether surprising that the draught should have left a cloud upon her memory. I went up to my room and got the letter, which I gave her without a word, and knelt by her chair as she turned the pages and read to the end, with slightly raised brows and eyes, in whose brightness there was no touch of softening.

'Rather a sentimental effusion!' she said at length. 'Am I expected to be responsible for it?'

'For God's sake don't sneer at it!' I exclaimed, on the verge of a flood of tears. 'It was written from the noblest and most generous impulse any woman could feel. I know it is all different now. I have lost your respect—you despise me—but, oh, Evelyn, don't abandon me altogether—don't take this away from me too! You promised—you promised. You *know* I cannot speak to him myself. And if you do not, he will go—and I shall die!'

'Need we be quite so tragic over this affair?' she said. 'I have never said that I was unwilling to carry out the promise in this letter. I have no animosity against you. On the contrary, I feel considerably indebted to you, as you may understand. And if this lover of yours is really so faint-hearted or so stupid as to need any encouragement from me, he shall have it. What do you wish me to tell him?'

'Tell him what you will,' I said, 'I am below pride now. Tell him that I love him with all my heart, as he loves me . . . Evelyn,' I broke off, as a sudden, terrible doubt struck me, 'you—you did not write this to mock me? You are sure he *does* love me? Is it true that he told you so with his own lips?'

'As true as that I wrote this letter,' she said, 'which, by the way, is not worth preserving,' and she tore it up as she spoke. 'Leave it to me, my dear. If there is anything I can do to bring about a better understanding between you and this Hugh Dallas it shall be done.'

I could not look into her candid eyes and doubt her any longer, I wondered how I could ever have felt even a passing distrust. I had disappointed her, shaken her faith in me, but hers was not the nature to allow that to affect her conduct. My future was as safe in her gentle hands as before.

'I ought to have known,' I said gratefully; 'you are too sweet and generous not to forgive. But you will tell him soon—will you not? You won't keep me or—or him longer in suspense than you can help?'

'Isn't he coming this afternoon?' she said lightly. 'I suppose I shall have an opportunity of seeing him then—and in the meantime, my dear, you must contrive to control your impatience.'

Hugh Dallas did come that afternoon, to find us sitting on the lawn in the shade, as on his first visit to Tansted. I thought him paler, and though we shook hands as if we had parted on the most ordinary and amicable terms, he avoided looking at me, preferring, it seemed, to read his answer in Evelyn's face rather than mine. But for this I was grateful, for I had been afraid that my countenance would betray me only too clearly.

It was evident that he was struck at once by her marvellous recovery of health and animation. I thought he gathered that it was of good omen for him, for he scarcely took his eyes from her face, and his own brightened.

'You look at me as if you had never seen me before!' she said laughing.

'I could almost believe some miracle had happened to you,' he replied. 'I certainly never saw you looking so wonderfully well before.'

'I feel as if I had been given a fresh lease of life,' she said. 'But if there has been anything miraculous about it, it is Stella you have to thank for it.'

'Miss Maberly?' he cried, and then he looked at me for the first time, and I saw anxiety, bewilderment, I know not what, conflict of hope and fear passing over his face, before I turned my eyes away.

He said something to her in so low a tone that it escaped me, but I gathered that she was playfully declining to enlighten him any further just then, and shortly afterwards tea was brought out and Mrs Maitland joined us, when he was obliged to wait for a more convenient moment.

I sat silent, but very happy, especially after I noted the eagerness with which he accepted Evelyn's invitation to dine at Tansted that evening. I knew that I should not have to be cruel to him or to myself very much longer.

I laughed inwardly when Mrs Maitland, under the transparent pretext of consulting me on the arrangement of the flowers at table, drew me into the house.

'I thought we would leave them to themselves a little, my dear,' she confided to me, 'because *this* time, I really think— This wonderful change in her, you know. Depend upon it, she has been fretting and making herself ill all this time because she couldn't make up her mind whether she cared enough for him—and now her last doubts have disappeared, her health and spirits have come back immediately. Last night was evidently the crisis.'

I humoured her, with a secret enjoyment of the surprise that awaited the unsuspecting lady, and of the very different result that she was so innocently helping to further, but I was only too glad to leave Hugh in Evelyn's hands. An hour or so later I watched him from my window riding down the avenue on his way home to dress, and thought I detected a buoyant hopefulness in the air with which he sat his horse.

He knew the truth now, or as much of it as Evelyn had thought fit to tell him; he understood at last that he need not fear another repulse from me.

How lovingly I lingered over dressing that evening, with a tender, unfamiliar delight in adorning myself for his eyes. I put on my prettiest gown; I felt a glad pride in the knowledge that I was looking even better than I could have hoped.

I was ready. I went across to Evelyn's room and found her standing before the long mirror. I was positively startled as I realised how wondrously lovely she was in her pale shimmering gown, her fair neck and shoulders set off by deep flounces of lace which fell over her breast and arms, one hand hovering like a white butterfly over her golden head as she gave the final touch to the ornament in her hair. I had never seen her look so bewitchingly beautiful; even the maid who stood by was staring at her in a sort of fascination.

When she had been sent out of the room, I went up to Evelyn and put my hands on her shoulders. 'Does he know?' I whispered. 'You have told him?'

She laughed. 'I could hardly tell him you were dying of love for him—could I, Stella? But I said as much as I could for you, and I fancy he is beginning to suspect that he has been extraordinarily blind. I should not be surprised if he found an opportunity of coming to a better understanding with you before long—'

'How can I thank you? I shall owe it all to you. And—I love him so much, Evelyn. If I could make you understand what it means to me?'

'My dear,' she said, 'I understand. You owe me nothing at all. And, as those are probably the wheels of his dog-cart[6] I hear, perhaps you will leave off crushing my poor lace and we will go downstairs.'

I was hoping that there would be something—a glance, a pressure of the hand—by which Hugh Dallas would convey to me when we met that he was conscious that the cloud between us had lifted, though, as I told myself the moment after, I might have guessed that delicacy would prevent him from seeming to take anything for granted until he had heard it from my own lips. It might have been my own fault, too, for I was oppressed then and throughout the dinner by the old constraint, which I was furious with myself for being unable to conquer.

I was horribly nervous, and he seemed scarcely less embarrassed; now and then I could see him glance at Evelyn with an air of appeal and almost reproach, as if he suspected that she had misled him by giving any encouragement.

But I am not sure that I did not find, before the meal came to an end, that the artificial constraint between us had a subtle charm of its own, which I would not have lost just yet. So soon now—perhaps before the last sunset gleam had quite died out of the sky—all misunderstanding would be removed; there was a piquancy in keeping up this pretence of coldness until the last moment, a delicious flattery in the sight of the suspense and anxiety from which he so evidently suffered.

And at last the moment came. Evelyn had proposed that we should go into the garden after dinner, and, linking her arm in Mrs Maitland's, she had contrived to draw her away to a distant part of the grounds, so as to give Hugh the opportunity she had promised. He was not slow in availing himself of it. He came over to the corner of the lawn in which I was sitting, drew up a chair beside mine, and sat down. For some little time he was silent, and, though I could scarcely see his face in the deepening shadow under the branches, I could tell that he was deeply moved.

I felt no impatience for him to speak; it was enough that he was there, close by me. I lay back in my chair in dreamy content. The western sky was passing from saffron to citron-green and deep luminous blue, the flower borders glowed dimly through the falling veil of dusk, the martins were flitting noisily in and out of their nests under the gables, a cricket chirped incessantly somewhere in the house, and the bats swooped and wheeled through the warm air, uttering tiny shrill cries. It all seemed a sort of peaceful prelude to the supreme hour at hand—the hour that was to bring me the full assurance of the love I had hungered for.

And presently he spoke, in a low voice which trembled and faltered at times, as if, even yet, he could hardly believe in his good fortune.

'Tell me,' he began, 'is it true—what I have heard this afternoon? That you are no longer my enemy, that, in spite of what happened yesterday afternoon, we are to be friends after all?'

'I—I never was your enemy, really,' I said. 'It was all a mistake. I —I misunderstood. I asked Evelyn to—to explain to you.'

'What can I say to you? You have made me very happy. If you knew what despair I was in last night—how little I thought that there was any hope of gaining your approval!'

'Forget yesterday,' I said softly, 'forget what I have been to you before you knew, only tell me that Evelyn has made you understand, that you really are the happier for it. I want to be quite, quite sure of that.'

And then he began to speak of Evelyn, and gradually, as he dwelt on her sweetness and fascination, a deadly suspicion stole over me that I was duping myself once more—that in some way Evelyn had played me false.

For some time I tried to think that I must have heard wrongly; nothing so hideous *could* be. I kept myself under control, and drew him on until I knew the truth.

I don't remember the exact form in which he conveyed it. He was very diplomatic; he did not say in so many words that his love for me had been a passing fancy, that he accepted his rejection as final, and was grateful to me for reading his heart more truly than he had known it himself. But that was what he made me understand, nevertheless. I had to hear how, in that single afternoon, Evelyn had beguiled and enslaved him utterly, how all his hopes now lay in winning her, and how he felt, notwithstanding, that there was some indefinable change in her attitude towards him which made him despair of touching her heart.

And I listened to all these rhapsodies of his—which were not for me. I listened and gave no sign of suffering, though the solid earth seemed sinking away beneath my feet, and the sky above the black tree tops to open and shut in livid fire; there was a loud ringing in my ears, and I found myself gripping the arms of my chair with such force that the bamboo splinters pierced the palms of my hands, and perhaps kept me from fainting, which was my dread.

No, I would not faint; he should not have the satisfaction of seeing that I cared; it was all over—whatever he had felt for me, he felt it no longer; whether Evelyn had deliberately fooled and betrayed me or not, it could make no difference, she had won him from me all the same—my short, mad, beautiful dream was dead now, and nothing, nothing would bring it back.

So I schooled myself to make such replies as were necessary. I spoke and even laughed once or twice, and my voice sounded quite naturally; or if there was a note of heartbreak at times, he was not likely to detect it. How should he, when his thoughts were so far from me?

I think I was glad when Mrs Maitland came towards us. 'Evelyn asked me to fetch her a cloak,' she said. 'Shall I bring you out yours too, Miss Maberly?'

'Thank you, no,' I said. 'I am quite happy and comfortable without it. And why should you go when I daresay Mr Dallas will take Evelyn her cloak and spare you the trouble.'

I had no desire to keep him there any longer. I believe I wanted to torture myself by seeing how eagerly he would accept a pretext for rejoining Evelyn, and if so, I was gratified.

'How good you are to me!' he said in an undertone, as he rose, and Mrs Maitland sank into the chair he had left and began to purr apologetically.

'It was really getting so late, my dear,' she said, 'I felt that it was time to do *something*. Dear Evelyn seems so strange to-night—this afternoon I was almost certain she had decided to take him, and now she has been positively neglecting him all this while. However, it's a comfort to see that you have got over your dislike to him—you seem to be quite good friends now?'

'Quite,' I said.

'It was so clever and sweet of you to understand my little hint about the cloak and send him to her.'

I looked across the lawn, and saw his indistinct form hastening to the spot where Evelyn's gown glimmered faintly through the gloom.

'He was only too glad to go,' I said.

'Yes, poor fellow, he is more hopelessly in love than ever—it is Evelyn I can't feel certain about. She has been talking so lightly

and capriciously about him, so unlike her usual self. Still I hope
and believe it will all end in the right way. And now she can feel
that he has *your* approval, it must have a great influence on her
—don't you think so, my dear?'

So Mrs Maitland flowed on in conjecture and comment, and
I sat and answered automatically, with an icy ache at my heart.

And yet, even then, I had not lost faith in Evelyn. She could not
have deliberately misled me. She would be horrified and indignant when she discovered the change in his feelings, she would
remonstrate with him, do all in her power to check and cure his
infatuation—perhaps, who knew? he would come back to me in
time.

So I longed to tell her everything and to have the assurance
that, if I had lost all else, her loyal and tender sympathy was still
left.

Later that evening, after Hugh Dallas had started to drive
home, the opportunity came. Mrs Maitland had gone upstairs,
leaving Evelyn and myself in the drawing-room. She was moving
about the room, restlessly taking up and replacing books and
knick-knacks, and singing little snatches of song under her
breath, with occasional side-glances at me of curiosity or challenge, until I could bear the suspense no longer.

'Sit down,' I cried; 'you know there is something we must talk
over together!'

'So late?' she said, 'and after such an exhausting evening! I
warn you, Stella, that if it is anything very serious I shall in all
probability fall asleep.'

She let herself sink gracefully into the nearest couch, with
her hands lightly linked behind her neck and her eyes gleaming
through their narrowed lids.

'It is serious enough for me,' I said; 'Evelyn, I have found out
to-night that Hugh doesn't love me any more—it is all over!'

'After proposing and being rejected—let me see—only yesterday, wasn't it? It seems an unusually rapid recovery. I'm afraid you
must have put your refusal in such plain words that his vanity was
too much for his passion.'

'I never meant to refuse him—you know all that was a mistake!'

'It is very unfortunate, but if he has chosen to take you at your word, I scarcely see what is to be done.'

'You promised to make him understand that—that—ah! you haven't told him!'

'He understands that you have reconsidered your disapproval of him and are ready to look upon him as a friend.'

'And was that all you told him?'

'Would you have had me tell him more when he was so obviously contented with less? I left it to you to attempt to relight his burnt-out fires, my dear, and I regret to find that you do not appear to have been successful, though you will do me the justice to admit that I gave you an excellent opportunity.'

'I did not try,' I said; 'he made me see that it was quite useless. Evelyn, he told me that it is you he loves now.'

'That is very interesting, though I'm afraid it is not such a surprise to me as it evidently is to you.'

'But you won't let him?'

'How can I prevent it? It is bad taste on his part, no doubt, but you have given him his liberty.'

'I did not know what I was doing. Evelyn, you *know* I never meant it. And I love him, I can't live without him. Ah, give him back to me.'

'Is it not just possible that he may not wish to be handed over?'

'It is not too late even yet,' I pleaded. 'You could make him come back if you would; if you only would!'

'Why should I? He happens to be quite the best-looking and most attractive person I have met for a long while; and if he pays me the compliment of falling in love with me, *I*, at all events; don't intend to reward him with frowns.'

'You have made him fall in love with you,' I said violently. 'You set yourself to bewitch him, to make him forget me. I trusted you and you betrayed me. Yes, I see that now!'

She unlaced her hands and leant forward with her eyes wide open and fixed on me with malicious mockery.

'Are you quite the person to reproach anybody with treachery?' she asked.

'What do you mean?' I stammered.

'Merely that I think I remember hearing only this morning of a person who, for reasons of her own, allowed, with full knowledge of the consequences, her dearest friend to be given a drug that would probably prove fatal.'

I shrank back under the gaze of those brilliant, malignant eyes. 'Evelyn,' I cried, 'as Heaven is my judge, I did not know, I did not think of the danger until it was too late.'

'*Qui veut la fin veut les moyens!*'[7] she said. 'If your conscience acquitted you, why did you accuse yourself of the crime as you did this morning?'

'You cannot be cruel enough to use my own words against me like that?' I said, trembling violently. 'Whatever I accused myself of in the state of mind I was in then, it went no further than a passing thought. How could it be called a crime when I did nothing?'

'I am not an authority on morals,' she said, 'but the distinction between actually administering a poison and allowing it to be given by another when a word would have prevented it, seems to me rather fine drawn. I'm afraid that, morally speaking, you must be considered a murderess, my dear Stella—a very charming and interesting one, I admit, but still a murderess.'

'You know I am not that. Why, you are better and stronger to-day than you have ever been—the chloral has done you no harm.'

'Me?' she said, smiling. 'None whatever. But that does not affect the main fact.'

I threw myself at her feet sobbing. 'Evelyn, I can't bear it. I can't—I can't. What has changed you like this, and made you hard and cynical when you were so forgiving and sweet only a few hours ago? Is it *I* who have done it all? For pity's sake, don't say these cruel, terrible things to me, not even if I have deserved them. I won't reproach you any more. I will own you are not to blame if Hugh has come to love you best. I give him up. I will be content, if only I have you. Be a little kind to me, Evelyn! Don't taunt and torture me with the past. Try to forgive me. Tell me that I have not lost the dearest, the only friend I had in the world. Be my own dear Evelyn once more!'

She thrust me away from her with a little gesture of petulant anger. 'Get up, Stella,' she said, 'why do you talk this nonsense to me? What is the use of pretences between us? Are you really such a fool as to try to deceive yourself? You know very well that I can never be your own dear Evelyn, as you call her, now; you know very well why—or,' she added, with a sudden peal of pitiless laughter, 'is it really possible that you have failed to grasp the situation yet? Is this ignorance of yours genuine? Let me look at your face and see.'

She seized my wrists in her light, cool grasp and attempted to draw me towards the lamplight.

'Let me go,' I cried, cowering with a sense that some nameless horror was before me. 'Don't look at me. Don't make me look at you. I am afraid. I am so afraid!'

'You fool!' she said angrily. 'You have nothing to fear from me. *I* am not your victim—the innocent, trustful girl whom you allowed to be drugged to death. You know what you found when you went in this morning.'

'It seemed to be death,' I said wildly. 'But it was not—it could not have been. And I prayed to God and He heard me.'

'God!' she answered contemptuously. '*God* does not hear such prayers as yours!'

'He did hear mine. He gave you back to me,' I insisted. 'If not, how should you be here?'

'Look at me,' she said, 'look me in the face—and then you will understand.'

I forced myself to lift my reluctant eyes to the lovely, scornful face that was looking down upon me—and then—God help me! I understood at last, and shrieked in an agony of despair and horror.

For in that awful moment I knew that it was not Evelyn's stainless soul that was gazing at me now through her eyes, but some evil, mocking spirit that my rash and blasphemous prayer had called to animate the form she had left.

And then the room seemed to grow dark suddenly, and with a loud rush and roar in my ears, and the hope that this might be death that was mercifully snatching me from those soft, cruel hands that held me so fast, I became insensible.

VI

When I recovered consciousness I found myself lying in bed in my own room. It was later than my usual hour for rising, and I felt dazed and confused. Someone had come in and drawn my curtains, for the sun was striking in on the cut-glass bottles on my dressing-table and making dancing prismatic flecks and bars on the ceiling and walls, at which I lay gazing with a languid sense of pleasure.

There was something reassuring in the pretty room and the wholesome sunlight, and though I had a vague recollection of having lately been through some awful experience, it was merely as of a dream too fantastically horrible to bear thinking of.

Presently there came a tap at my door, and I heard Evelyn's voice asking if she might come in. She entered, looking so fresh and fair that I wondered why my heart sank at the sound of her voice, and why the sight of her filled me with an almost ungovernable terror.

'I have brought you some breakfast,' she said, as she set down the tray. 'We didn't like to disturb you before, as you seemed to be sleeping so soundly. I hope you are quite recovered by this time.'

'I—I have had a bad night, I think,' I said, 'but I have not been ill—have I?'

She smiled. 'Then you have forgotten how you alarmed me, and, indeed, the whole house, by suddenly fainting in the drawing-room last night. I had to call Aunt Lucy and have you carried upstairs. Did you fancy you saw something that frightened you, Stella, or how was it? I saw nothing in the room but our two selves.'

I looked at her and saw that, in spite of her assumed innocence and unconsciousness, her eyes were watching my face uneasily. And then the whole scene came back to me, and I turned from her, shuddering.

'Ah, I remember,' I cried. 'My God, it was no dream—it is true,

true! I know you now—you are not my Evelyn—don't touch me, don't come near me.'

'Why, my dearest Stella,' she said soothingly, 'what does all this mean? What extraordinary idea has taken hold of you? You must be dreaming still. Who else should I be but Evelyn?'

I saw at once that she was anxious to undo the effect of her revelation last night, and persuade me that I had imagined it all —as if that was possible!

'I do not know who you are,' I said, 'but you are not Evelyn— nothing you can say will ever make me believe that again. Evelyn is dead and I am to blame, and you—fiend, devil, evil spirit, whatever you may be—have taken her form to torment me. But I will have no dealings with you, do you hear? You cannot compel me to accept you as—as what you only seem. I will not breathe the same air with you.'

Her mouth quivered pathetically, she looked sweetly grieved. 'Why do you treat me as if I were your enemy?' she asked softly, 'why should I wish to harm you, and what reason have you for even assuming that I am wicked at all?'

'Will you dare to pretend that you are Evelyn Heseltine?' I said; 'it will be useless, after what you said last night!'

'As you please,' she said. 'I am *not* Evelyn Heseltine, then. What am I? That is not so easy to say. Not so very long ago I was a human being, living my life on this earth, in this very England. I do not claim to have been a saint—if I had been a better woman my soul would not have been within hearing of your call. Thanks to your prayer, I was released from the penance that such as I must undergo, permitted to return to this dear, warm, beautiful world. I am young, I seem to be rich, I am good to look at, and I owe all this to you. Think whether I am likely to be ungrateful, whether, whatever I have been in the past, I may not be willing to avoid laying up worse punishment for myself in the future. I am ready to be your friend, and you repulse me as if I were some evil thing.'

'You *are* evil!' I cried. 'I feel it—all your fair words, all your sweet looks cannot deceive me. Say what you please, I will have nothing to do with you.'

'Are you so ungrateful, Stella?' she murmured reproachfully; 'when you owe me so much!'

'Ungrateful! What have I to be grateful to you for?' I asked.

'Much, I should have imagined. What would be your position now if I had not come to your rescue? Your friend would be lying dead in that room there, you would be under suspicion, at all events, of having had some share in her death—you seem to have allowed your jealousy and resentment to be apparent enough. At the best, you would be thrown on the world, penniless, and with a cloud hanging over your name. Whereas, who can accuse you, who can suspect you now, who will ever guess that I am not the real Evelyn—unless, of course, you are mad enough to suggest it to them?'

Still I tried to break through the meshes of cajolery in which I felt I was being entangled. 'I will say nothing,' I said, 'but I cannot live on here in this house with you. I will go away. I must.'

'I cannot do without you, Stella,' she said. 'This new existence which you—*you*, remember—have summoned me into, is still strange and unfamiliar. I want a guide, someone to instruct me in all it is necessary to know about myself, or I shall make blunders which, if they don't betray our little secret, will certainly set people speculating and gossiping. No, for your own sake you must stay with me.'

'Stay,' I cried, 'stay and lend myself to such a ghastly mockery! —oh, how can I, how can I?'

'Of course you can,' she said, 'and of course you will—there is nothing else to be done. Come, Stella,' she added more gently, 'we cannot undo the past, either you or I, so let us make the best of it. Don't harden your foolish heart against me any more. Trust yourself to me, you will not find me hard or cruel so long as you do your best to please me. What we two alone know will only link us closer together—in time you will even come to forget that I am not your own Evelyn. I can make you love me better than ever you loved her, if only you will let me try. Tell me that we are to be friends.'

I could not resist her any longer. I felt so utterly helpless, the situation was so terrible, that I caught at any compromise. I told myself that she *might* have spoken the truth, she might have come to save me. I could almost believe that it was Evelyn's very self that was pleading with me for my love and confidence. And so I yielded; I let her fold me in her arms and kiss me on the lips with a fierce possession that made me shiver.

'Now you are my own Stella,' she whispered caressingly. 'We understand one another, do we not? We are allies from this moment.'

Unnatural and unholy as such a compact was, it brought me a delusive comfort just then. If only she would be kind, if she could indeed make me forget even for a time, was it not as much as I could hope for now?

As soon as I had come downstairs, Evelyn—(for though it is repugnant to me to use that beloved name in connection with the spirit that had taken her form, I find myself compelled to do so)—Evelyn insisted that, as I was now quite recovered, I should accompany her on a round of inspection of the gardens and stables.

I knew that she wanted me to instruct her in all the details of an existence necessarily still unfamiliar to her, and I submitted passively, feeling all the while that I was sinking to the level of an accomplice.

She was extraordinarily quick in turning all my answers to account; not one of the servants we met, and whom she spoke to, suspected for a moment that she was anything but the young mistress they adored. Nothing untoward happened until we entered the stables, where Roy, Evelyn's favourite collie, was lying in his kennel.

At the first sight of her he had sprung forward to the full length of his chain, barking with delight, but as she came nearer I saw the dog's manner suddenly change, his bark died away into a terrified whine, his hair bristled, and he retreated before her, growling and showing his fangs.

I noticed Evelyn's colour change, though she showed no sign of fear. 'He seems very strange to-day,' she said quietly, as the collie slunk into his kennel, where he lay snarling. 'What can be the matter with him?' she asked Reynolds, the coachman, who happened to come out at that moment.

'I haven't noticed anything, Miss Evelyn,' he said. 'For the Lord's sake keep back, miss!' he cried the next instant, as she was about to go up and pat the dog's head, 'he means mischief, sure enough.'

He had just time to seize her arm and draw her out of reach as the dog made a sudden spring. Had the chain not been a strong one, nothing could have saved her from being torn to pieces.

'Come away,' I cried to her; 'come—before he breaks free.'

She stood there just beyond his reach, calmly looking down on the furious animal as it strove again and again to fly at her throat. 'You go,' she replied, 'if you are afraid to stop. I am quite able to take care of myself.'

I was afraid—terribly afraid; the effect which her presence produced upon the collie, as gentle and good-tempered a creature in ordinary[8] as ever breathed, came home to me like a rebuke. I could not bear it and fled back to the garden.

There Evelyn joined me later. 'Why, Stella, you are actually trembling still. What a coward you are! What is there to be so afraid of?'

'The dog knew,' I answered hoarsely. 'What is the use of my being silent? You will never silence *him*.'

'He is quiet enough now,' she replied. 'Come and see for yourself.'

Wondering what strange spell she could have used to subdue the animal so soon, I let her lead me back to the stable-yard, and there one glance at the dog, as he lay on his side with glazed eyes and protruded tongue, told me that he was silenced only too effectually.

'It is done, then?' she said to Reynolds, who was standing gloomily by the body. 'I hope the poor creature suffered no pain?'

'No, Miss Evelyn,' said the coachman. 'I gave him some proosic acid[9] as was put by in the harness room. He went off quite quiet, miss. He licked my hand as I gave him the stuff,' the man added, with a catch in his voice, for he had been fond of the dog. 'He seemed himself again the minute you'd gone, Miss Evelyn. I can't account for his breaking out as he did nohow—I can't. 'Taint as if he'd shown any sign of it afore.'

'He would never have flown at me like that unless he had been mad, quite dangerously mad,' said Evelyn. 'I am dreadfully grieved that it should have been necessary to have him put out of the way, but it was too great a risk to run, was it not, Stella?'

Her eyes shone with the sweetest pity, her tone would have sounded to most ears only tender and womanly, and yet on mine the words fell with a suggestion of hideous hypocrisy. They seemed to bear a covert menace addressed to me alone.

And from that moment all the old repulsion and dread which she had so nearly lulled awoke once more with an intensity that turned me sick and faint. Yes, it was in vain to delude myself any longer. Whatever spirit this might be that wore Evelyn's shape, looked at me with her fair eyes and spoke in her sweet voice, I knew now that it was altogether evil—a thing essentially false, cunning and relentless.

And I, miserable woman that I was, I was committed to this alliance. I was paralysed by the conviction that if I ventured to thwart or oppose her, she would make me feel her power in some terrible form that would plunge me into yet deeper misery and subjection.

VII

I had thought the loss of Hugh Dallas's love, at the very moment when I believed it won, the greatest misery that could befall me, but beside the overwhelming horror of such a secret as I now had to bear, his desertion seemed almost insignificant.

There were times when the thought that the gentle girl who had loved me was dead through my own half-guilty inaction, that some lost and wandering soul, if not a spirit from Hell itself, was masquerading in her form, and I was compelled to assist in this ghastly mockery, was so intolerable that it seemed as if my brain must inevitably give way under it.

Then I would try to persuade myself that my terrors were unreal, that I was the victim of some morbid hallucination which caused me to distort the most ordinary events, to find confirmation of my fancies in Evelyn's most innocent acts and speeches, and these attempts sometimes almost succeeded. She did everything in her power to overcome my antipathy, and there was a subtle witchery now in her looks and ways that made it hard to resist her always. I did so long to believe, if I only could, that she was just her own sweet human self, and not what my instinct and reason knew her to be.

I fancy that at the beginning she really had a kind of fierce, perverse fondness for me, or at least that she desired to conquer my affection and make a fascinated, submissive slave of me.

But that she could not do; my dread of her was too deeply rooted, it returned in spite of myself and made me as rebellious as I dared. And so it was not long before she realised that the aversion she inspired in me was proof against all her advances, and from that time she felt nothing for me but malignant hatred.

This showed itself especially in the systematic persecution she practised upon me whenever Hugh Dallas was with us, a torture so refined that no observer could have detected its insidious cruelty. For then she would overwhelm me with hypocritical caresses and little affectionate speeches which I was powerless either to resent or to respond to, except by what, as she knew perfectly well, would strike him as sullen ungraciousness. Or she would try to provoke me into some outbreak by apparently innocent remarks and allusions, so skilfully worded that I alone felt their sting.

Is it any wonder if sometimes these diabolical tactics of hers succeeded, and if under the strain I forgot all my prudent resolves to keep calm, to avoid playing into her hands by some violent retort which would merely put me more hopelessly in the wrong?

Occasionally, as I surprised her pathetic *moue*[10] of distress at my hardness of heart, and his answering look of sympathy and admiration of her angelic forbearance, or when I noted the alteration in his tone to me, his grave concern at my insensibility and incredulous wonder that any person could resist such sweetness as hers, occasionally a sense of a certain ghastly humour in the situation would seize me, and I would burst out laughing— hollow and mirthless laughter though it was—in his astonished face, which no doubt lowered his opinion of me more than ever.

I knew well enough that every scene of this sort left him more enraptured with Evelyn's incomparable excellence, more devoutly thankful for his lucky escape from such a warped and soured nature as mine, and I almost, if not quite, hated him for such infatuation, such blindness.

To him she was a pure and saintly being whom he felt unworthy to approach with earthly passion; he never saw, as I saw, that each shy, soft glance of hers, each dainty posture and slow, undulating movement was deliberately and cunningly calculated to increase the sensuous, intoxicating effect she produced.

It was bitter enough to be condemned to bear all this, and yet there was just one hope which sustained me. Such a nature as hers must be incapable of love; she could not be anything but indifferent to him; she would not have gone on playing with his feelings so long except for the pleasure she found in seeing how it tormented me. If I only restrained myself she would tire of her amusement in time, tire of her saintly pose, tire of his reverence and devotion, she would reveal herself to him as she really was—false, corrupt, cynical, cruel, and he was hardly the man whose love would survive such a shattering of his ideal. And if it did not, who could tell what might happen? He might come back to me—even yet.

I did not know myself how desperately I wished him to come back. I thought I hated and despised him too much to care now whether he did or not—it was only when this last poor hope was taken from me that I realised how much I had come to depend on it.

One evening, after Hugh Dallas had gone, Evelyn came into the room where I was sitting, knelt by my chair and turned her pleading face up to mine with an expression of such exaltation and tenderness and purity that for the moment I could again have almost believed that, in some wonderful way, my own dear Evelyn was restored to me.

But only for a moment—for, even as I gazed into those deep and lustrous eyes of hers, I saw the cunning, malignant devil I feared lurking there still, and I knew that some new scheme was on hand and that I must be on my guard.

'I've come to tell you something,' she began, and the pretty shyness and timidity in her voice and looks would assuredly have deceived anyone but me. 'Be kind to me now, Stella, don't be hard and bitter when I am so happy—so very, very happy. You will guess why, I think.... Hugh has asked me to be his wife.'

'His wife!' I cried. 'But you have not said yes? Don't tell me you have said that.'

'But I have, Stella. What else *could* I say, when I love him with all my heart? Why, I thought,' she added with the most perfect assumption of unconsciousness, 'I thought you no longer disliked him. I hoped you would be just a little glad!'

'You hoped no such thing. You know as well as I that the very name of love is a lie and a mockery on such lips as yours.'

She looked plaintive, bewildered. 'I don't understand you, Stella. You can't really mean such a cruel speech?'

'Oh, why do you play this comedy of innocence now?' I cried impatiently. 'You have no audience here to be deceived by it. It is all wasted on me. Let us speak plainly now we are alone. Understand this: I will not stand by and permit such a marriage as this. Do what you will to me—and even you cannot make me much more miserable than I am!—I will prevent you from blighting Hugh Dallas's life.'

It was curious to see how, though obviously uneasy at the opposition she had roused in me, she still tried to keep up her assumed character. 'You are not yourself,' she said. 'Stella, dear Stella, try not to give way to these moods; they—they frighten me.'

'If they do,' I said, 'so much the better. Be warned, for I mean what I say. Unless you give up this wicked design of yours, I will tell Hugh what you are, let it cost me what it will. He shall know that it is not Evelyn's spotless soul that makes her form seem so wondrously fair, but a devil—a vile and fiendish spirit that has taken possession of her lifeless shell.'

She made no reply, but retreated a step or two and stood gazing at me with dilated eyes. I believe that, for the moment at all events, she really was alarmed, and so I left her, feeling that for once the advantage was with me.

Fool that I was to suppose that I was any match for her! That same night she glided into my room and stood by my bedside, like some lovely apparition in her white robe and with her fair hair floating loose about her shoulders. She bent over me in the attitude of a guardian angel and laid her soft, cool palm on my burning forehead, but the mocking curve of her lips and the sinister glitter in her eyes told me that the mask was dropped, and my heart sank with a slavish dread.

'You were very bold, Stella,' she said in a soft, deliberate whisper. 'Your threats sounded quite determined, and yet, you know and I know that you will never carry them out—no, you will never find the courage to enlighten Hugh Dallas. What can you hope to gain by it?'

'I should save him from you,' I said.

'Your hopes go farther than that. You are still clinging to the idea that if he knew me as I am he would come back to you. You cannot deceive me, you see. But have you reflected that you cannot convince him of what *I* am without confessing what *you* are? Are you really sanguine enough to believe that, though he is utterly indifferent to you now, his passion will revive when he sees you in your new character—a jealous, treacherous murderess, compelled to conceal her guilt by accepting such help as mine?'

'I am not a murderess—he will never believe that of me.'

'Oh, no, he will not believe it, he will not believe a single word of your confession, denunciation, whatever you prefer to call it. He will merely regard it as an exhibition of hysterical spite and jealousy; his masculine vanity will be tickled by the discovery that you are still passionately in love with him. He will pity you, perhaps, but he will certainly despise you. Will you be satisfied then?'

'He shall never pity me!' I cried. 'And you are wrong. I love him no longer. I hate him—yes, I hate him!'

'And yet you would try to save him from me? It is not as if you would succeed. You would only humble yourself in vain. He would think—you can imagine what he would think of you! But there, I am not afraid of you, Stella—you have too much pride to make yourself contemptible in his eyes for nothing. You are passionate, too; you would like to see this man suffer as he has made you suffer. Leave him in my hands and I will avenge you. Do you think he will be happier or better for loving me? Could you wish for a more complete revenge than to see this faithless lover of yours kneeling at my feet?'

'I do not want revenge,' I said. 'I do not want Hugh to suffer.'

'Then you are more superhumanly magnanimous than I gave

you credit for being,' she said. 'But whether that is so or not, it comes to the same thing in the end. Hugh Dallas is mine, and you will not interfere between us; you have neither the courage nor the power—nor even the will. To-morrow you will have come to your senses, you will keep a strict guard over yourself, and behave both to Hugh and me as if you entirely approved of our engagement and heartily rejoiced in the happiness of your dearest friend. That is what I came to say to you, my beloved Stella, and, now it is said, I will leave you in peace.'

She gave me a cruel little kiss, as though in half-contemptuous acknowledgment of my submission, and was gone, noiselessly and ghost-like as she had come in.

And the next morning I did exactly as she had predicted. She was all gentleness and affection, and when I began to refer to the scene between us the night before, entreated me to forget it. Everything was forgotten and forgiven, and I was her own dear Stella again.

I had to listen and respond to Mrs Maitland's ecstasies at the fulfilment of her dearest wishes, which she evidently imagined she had brought about by her own diplomacy. I had to see Hugh Dallas arrive in all the pride and glory of an accepted suitor. I even congratulated him, and I believe without betraying by voice or manner the horrible suffering it cost me.

The news of the engagement seemed to give general satisfaction. Hugh was popular in the county, and Whinstone society was full of praises of Evelyn's beauty and sweetness and charm. No one for a moment suspected the secret change in her. She played her part with such consummate skill that, as I have already said, even I was sometimes tempted to an involuntary forgetfulness of the ghastly reality. And so for days I stood by and held my peace, despising myself for my cowardice, and yet powerless to utter even a hint of what I knew, until at last something happened which loosened my tongue in spite of every reason for prudence and self-restraint.

Hugh had heard, of course, of the narrow escape which Evelyn had had from being bitten by Roy, and with the over-anxiety of a lover had made her promise—he little knew how superfluous such a precaution was—that she would not have another collie.

By way, I suppose, of a safer substitute, he had offered to get her a Blenheim,[11] and one afternoon when he drove over he brought with him a tiny liver and white spaniel, which he presented to her in the garden.

I was with her at the time and noticed, with a thrill of secret gratification, the look of chagrin and dismay on her face when the little creature cowered away from her endearments with every sign of abject terror. 'He won't come to me, Hugh,' she exclaimed, glancing up at him with piteous eyes and quivering lips, like a child on the brink of tears. 'Look, he declines to have anything to do with me.'

Hugh laughed and said something about all dogs being shy at first. 'Beau will very soon discover that he is a very fortunate animal,' he said.

I felt strangely irritated by this denseness of his; perhaps, too, the sight of the horror with which the animal shrank from her touch filled me with shame at my own more cowardly submission; at all events, I could not keep back the words which rushed to my lips.

'You are wrong, Mr Dallas,' I said. 'Evelyn will never succeed in persuading that creature to trust her or be friendly with her. Dogs have instincts of their own, and are not to be deceived even by her.'

I saw the indignation and surprise in his handsome face, the sudden change in hers, and I went on recklessly: 'He hates you, Evelyn, he sees more clearly than others—though he is only a dog. But perhaps you will call him mad, too, like poor Roy, whom you had put out of the way. Yes, Mr Dallas, I warn you not to leave that dog here. He will not live long in this house—she will take care of that!'

He raised his eyebrows as he looked at her with a sort of troubled inquiry, and then he answered me quietly and compassionately, as if he were humouring a fractious child.

'Come, Miss Maberly,' he said, 'you don't really believe what you say. You know perfectly well that Beau could not be in kinder hands than Evelyn's, and that she is incapable of harming any living thing. Why do you give way to such extravagant ideas? See how unhappy you are making her.'

'If I could make her as wretched as she makes me,' I cried, maddened by his tone, 'but then—what is the use of saying any more? You *will* not see. By-and-by, when it is too late, perhaps, you will remember that I tried to warn you.'

And I left them standing there pale and mute, and I knew that it would be some time before either of them recovered their equanimity.

When Hugh went away that evening, Beau made a desperate attempt to follow, and refused to be comforted for his former master's desertion. Curiously enough, for I have no natural inclination to purely useless pets, it was to me that he came for protection, and I was so far touched by the poor beast's confidence that I insisted on keeping it with me for the night at least, since it would not allow Evelyn to touch it.

In its dumb, foolish way it loved Hugh, and perhaps, even though I told myself that I hated him now, that gave it a certain claim upon me.

I took it up to my room and it slept there at the foot of my bed, where, as I lay awake through the night, I listened for its soft breathing, and even now and then bent forward to touch its smooth, silken head and assure myself that it was still there and safe.

And at daybreak I woke from a short and troubled sleep with a sense that evil eyes were looking down on me—and when I looked Evelyn was standing there.

'Do you know you were very imprudent yesterday, you poor, impulsive Stella?' she began softly. 'You ought to have discovered by this time that it is unwise to try to defy *me*. I really think you deserve some slight punishment, just as a lesson to avoid these indiscretions for the future. Was it quite wise to warn Hugh that this little creature'—she laid one white hand lightly on the spaniel, which moaned and shivered in his sleep—'would never consent to make friends with me?'

'Whether it was wise or not to say it, it was the truth. You know it was true,' I said.

'You went further than that,' she said. 'You hazarded a prediction that the animal would not live long if left to my tender mercies. You would probably not be sorry to see your anticipation fulfilled, like most prophets of evil.'

'What do you mean?' I cried. 'My God! What are you going to do?'

'Only to convince our excellent Hugh of your skill in prophecy,' she said, and with that she seized the wretched spaniel, and deliberately strangled it before my eyes. I lay there, too paralysed by horror and pity to move or cry out; I could only look on as the poor little life ebbed slowly away between those slender, pitiless hands.

'You devil!' I cried at last, when all was over and the victim dropped, limp and still, from her grasp. 'You cruel, malicious devil! Hugh shall hear of this—everyone shall know. Thank God, you have overreached yourself this time—you have shown yourself as you really are!'

She laughed with an infernal glee and triumphant wickedness, which made my blood run chill.

'You are too hasty, as usual, my dearest Stella. It is not I who have overreached myself. If you reflect for a moment, you will see that you are the only person who can possibly be connected with this incident. It was *you* who foretold that the dog would come to a tragic end; you who, though you avowedly dislike such creatures, took him up into your own room; you who have made no secret of your jealousy of me and your hatred of Hugh. What more natural than that in a sudden burst of frenzy you should have carried out your own prediction? Who will suspect harmless, innocent Evelyn Heseltine? Why, you fool, I shall come down in a few hours, having slept peacefully all night, and utterly ignorant that any harm has happened to the dog that was given me only yesterday by my beloved Hugh. If you accuse me, do you know what will be said? Everyone—Hugh and all—will think that you are insane, mad with disappointed love and jealous brooding. 'Such a pity—a beautiful, spirited girl like poor Miss Maberly—most distressing case—such a shock to her friend, Miss Heseltine, who was absolutely devoted to her—but really for everybody's sake it would be better if some steps were taken.' Can't you hear the good folk of Whinstone gossiping? And all your own doing—you thought you could match yourself against me, and you see you have failed!'

I recognised the frightful truth in what she said. Appearances were all in her favour and against me. Devil that she was she had me at her mercy, and I had no choice but to submit.

'I know,' I said, know it is useless for me to contend against you. If—if I keep silence, if I tell nobody that you did this thing, you will not let the blame fall upon me? I *could* not bear him—or anyone—to think me capable of such horrible cruelty!'

'I should have imagined,' she said, 'that this was the merest trifle compared to the charge that *might* be brought against you. It is nothing to me whether you accuse me or not—you will only injure yourself. Still, as you seem to have learnt your lesson, you shall be helped out of the difficulty for once. If you like to tell me at breakfast that your *protégé* had a fit during the night and died, I shall be too simple-minded and guileless to doubt your story, and there will be no questions asked or fuss of any kind. That is what, in your own interests, I should advise you to do—but of course you will follow your own judgment.'

I know it was a despicable surrender—and yet, what else could I do? Anything seemed better just then than the thought of having to endure Hugh's scorn and loathing as a monster of cruelty, or—which was even worse—being shunned as a mad-woman.

It was hard to believe that the girl I met at the breakfast-table that morning, so fair and fresh and dainty, could have possibly committed that cold-blooded act a few hours before.

I told the tale she had suggested, though it sounded lame and unconvincing enough, and I feared that Mrs Maitland's suspicions must be excited by my manner.

But for Evelyn I think they would have been, but she came to my assistance, as she had promised, and after the first well-feigned outburst of surprise and distress and pity, she contrived to convince the elder lady that the spaniel's death was due to purely natural causes, and to make her understand that I was not well enough just then to be worried about what was probably a pain-ful and disagreeable experience, and so the matter passed over.

Mrs Maitland had not heard my reckless warning to Hugh about the danger of leaving the dog in Evelyn's hands, so that she was the less likely to see any significance in its speedy death.

I was not present when Evelyn told Hugh. I dreaded lest I

might see in his face that he suspected me, and I could not have borne that.

Still, I trusted that Evelyn would remove any suspicions he might have. It did not enter my head then that she would be vile and false enough to encourage or much less suggest them.

But, as the days went on, I became aware of a change in his manner to me, a repressed aversion which he had certainly never shown before. I could see quite plainly that he disliked to see Evelyn with me, though he might have discovered from my cowed, spiritless bearing, if he had cared, how hateful and heavy I found my yoke.

I knew by a sort of instinct that she was playing me false. She was filling his mind with lying impressions, and I was determined to find out how much she had told him, how far he believed her.

So I watched my opportunity of being alone with him, and then I challenged him pointblank.

'Mr Dallas, I have noticed that you have been different to me of late. Don't trouble to deny it. I know it perfectly well, and I know the reason. Evelyn has been saying things against me.'

'Evelyn is not given to speaking or thinking unkindly of anyone she loves.'

'That is not an answer. She does not love me. What has she been telling you?'

'Why do you harbour such thoughts? Don't you see that you are making your life a misery?'

'My life is made a misery, but not by me.'

'It's sheer perversity,' he said. 'You could conquer these ideas of yours if you only made an effort, but if you insist on seeing enemies in those who care for you——'

'No one cares for me now,' I said. '*You* did once, or thought you did for a time, until she came between us.'

He chose to ignore—perhaps she had actually made him forget—that there had ever been a time when he believed that he loved me. 'That's nonsense,' he said shortly, though his manner prevented the words from seeming brutal. 'I am as ready to be your friend now as ever I was—*more* ready, indeed; and so, as you ought to know very well, is Evelyn, whom you are doing everything you can to make miserable.'

'I was sure of it,' I cried. 'She *has* been talking to you about me! Mr Dallas, has she dared to tell you that—that it was I who killed your poor Beau? It is a lie!'

'Good heavens!' he exclaimed. 'Who accuses you of any such thing? Not Evelyn—nor I!'

'But you *suspect* me of it. You know you do! I warned you that he would not live long here. And it was in my room that he died!'

'Was it?' he said, as if I could not see that he knew it perfectly well. 'I did not know. And if so, what of it? There's no earthly reason why you should make yourself unhappy about that—no one supposes that you are responsible.'

'There it is! You don't consider me responsible for my actions! Evelyn has been telling you I am not. You believe that I am—*mad*!'

He made a gesture of angry despair. 'How you twist the most ordinary words! I do not believe you are mad. If I did, it would be some excuse for you. But you are quite able to control yourself if you only choose. You *must* make the effort, Miss Maberly. Throw off these morbid fancies of yours and you will see Evelyn as she really is—a loving, devoted friend, who wishes nothing but your happiness.'

His tone was gentler; he looked so honest and wholesome-minded, so manly and gallant, as he stood there that I could not find it in my heart to hate him any longer, if I ever had really hated him for his faithlessness to me. I could not even despise him for his blind belief in her; a great pity came over me, a longing to save him, if I could, from what he was drifting to.

'My happiness!' I cried. 'Ah, my God! if you knew—if I dared to tell you—but I am afraid. You would not listen to what I said—you would only tell *her*!'

'If there is anything on your mind which it would be a relief to tell me, you may trust me not to speak of it—even to Evelyn.'

'I *will* tell you!' I cried; 'I can't bear it any longer. You shall know what this Evelyn who has bewitched you into loving her really is, whatever she makes me suffer for it.'

'That is enough,' he interrupted sternly. 'I thought you wished to tell me something that concerned yourself. You don't suppose I shall listen to any wild charges against her. If you are sincere, and really believe that poor Evelyn is a cruel tyrant, and the Lord only knows what else, why, in Heaven's name, don't you free yourself—why do you stay here at Tansted?'

'Because I must,' I said. 'I have begged her to let me go away, but she will not.'

'I will undertake that you are allowed to go if you wish it,' he replied. 'Anything would be better than this wretched state of affairs.'

'You want to get rid of me!' I said bitterly. 'You do not care what becomes of me—it is nothing to you that I have nowhere else to go.'

'You need not be afraid of being turned out into the world to shift for yourself,' he replied. 'Evelyn would see that your future was provided for. If she once understands that you are miserable in this house, and that nothing she can do will ever overcome the bitterness you have allowed yourself to feel towards her, she will agree with me that it is better for your happiness that you should leave her as soon as possible.'

It was humiliating, weak, inconsistent enough, I know, and yet I suddenly recognised that I could endure anything, even the secret torture, the consuming fever of jealousy and dread and impotent hate that were now my portion, rather than be banished from the only place where I could ever see and speak to Hugh Dallas. Besides, where could I go and hope for peace of mind? Where could I even be sure of being safe from her?

'Mr Dallas,' I said, 'I—I did not mean all I said just now. I *will* try to behave differently to Evelyn, if—if only you will not say anything to her. You—you don't know what harm you would do me if you told her that I had been complaining.'

'I will say nothing,' he replied, 'but you must understand this: I will not have Evelyn worried and distressed by any more of these violent scenes and reproaches. Unless you can control these unreasonable tempers and make a better return for the affection and forbearance she shows you, your stay here must and shall end.'

'Make your mind easy, Mr Dallas,' I said. 'You have shown me how mistaken I have been. I shall keep a stricter guard over my tongue for the future.'

'That's right,' he replied cordially; 'or rather, keep your mind from brooding over these fanciful wrongs of yours and you won't need to curb your tongue. There, Miss Maberly, I'm quite sure you won't oblige me to lecture you like this again—you are going to be sensible; let us shake hands over it.'

'Yes, I am going to be sensible, I will give no more trouble,' I said, and I gave him my hand and he held it in his firm warm one for just a second or so, and I turned away with an aching heart at the thought that this calm, friendly interest was all he would ever feel for me now.

I had done my best; I had tried to warn him of his danger, and it was useless. If I overcame my dread of Evelyn and attempted once more to open his eyes, I should only incur his anger as well as hers. I should only be rewarded by seeing his endeavours to drive me away.

He would not let me save him, and so I could only leave him in his blindness. For the remainder of that day I compelled myself to make more response to Evelyn's simulated affection, and I hoped that she would not find out my attempt to defy and thwart her.

But though I am quite certain that it was not Hugh who betrayed me, she knew nevertheless, and taunted me with my failure that very night in one of those stealthy visits of hers, which thenceforward made me dread the approach of darkness and the mockery of lying down to rest.

For she would come almost every night now, in the small hours before daybreak, and sit by my pillow and whisper the most appalling threats and gibes in my reluctant ear. I did not dare to lock my door against her, and if I had, I knew that it would be but a vain protection. I tried to close my ears, but she caught my hands and held them fast, and I was forced to listen.

She would tell me with dreadful triumph that, though I was sane as yet, it would not be long before, thanks to her, I should be driven across the narrow line that still divided me from madness. She would declare what I had been hitherto unaware of, and do not even now believe—that my own mother had died in a private asylum, and that I should inevitably come to the same end. Or she would recall every act or speech of mine during the previous day that was capable of being distorted into evidence of mental disease, and gloat over my progress towards insanity.

Then she delighted in repeating all Hugh's tender and ador-
ing speeches to her, and every slighting or compassionate remark
he and others had made about myself. And other things worse
still—things the stain of which I would willingly wash from my
memory if I could—she would murmur in caressing musical
tones that made them the more hideous to hear.

All this, as she openly avowed, was deliberately done to render
me gradually insane through mental anguish and loss of sleep,
and it would hardly have been wonderful if her diabolical scheme
had succeeded, and if, after a night of relentless persecution such
as this, I had indeed broken forth the next day in some fashion
that might seem madness to most ears.

But I knew how fatal that would be, and I was resolved not to
gratify her hatred by any loss of self-command that I could possibly help. No one but myself ever knew how near I came to it
at times, when I felt the blood surging and boiling up into my
brain, and the control of speech and thought slipping, slipping
away from me.

It was hard to have to endure Evelyn's falseness, to notice the
ostentatious pains she took in public to humour or calm me, to
isolate me as much as possible from local society, while secretly,
as I knew only too well, she was encouraging the idea that my
mind was unhinged. When I went amongst people now I could
see they looked askance at me. I could almost hear their whispers,
and I was often sorely tempted to go up and ask them plainly why
they were afraid of me, and give the lie boldly to the rumours
that Evelyn had been treacherously spreading.

Still, I resisted all such impulses, feeling very certain that they
would only answer me with smooth evasions or polite, lying
denials, and then I might indeed have been stung into violent passion, which, of course, would be exactly what Evelyn hoped to
effect.

VIII

The day fixed for the wedding, which was to be early in September, came nearer and nearer; presents poured in; arrangements

for feasting Hugh Dallas's tenantry and the Whinstone school children and poor were discussed and decided on, and though I could not help being aware of all this, I remained passive. Somehow I could not persuade myself that this iniquitous union would really take place.

One Sunday morning, however, the fancy seized me that I would go to church once more and try whether I might gain some little comfort and strength to endure my daily and hourly temptations and the torture of my nightly ordeal, and, for a wonder, I had been allowed to go, though not without Mrs Maitland as a keeper and spy over me.

For a time the familiar rhythm and wording of the noble liturgy, the rise and fall of the intoning, and the hearty ring of the responses, exercised a soothing effect upon me; I felt safe and comparatively at peace, content to trust the future in the hands of the God whom we were imploring to have mercy upon us, and who seemed so near and so ready to listen to our prayers just then.

And then suddenly I heard that which roused my drugged conscience and convinced me that action and not weak, cowardly resignation was required of me. The rector was publishing the banns of marriage between Hugh Dallas and Evelyn Heseltine for the third time, and as he uttered the solemn adjuration to any of us who knew cause or just impediment why those two persons should not be joined together in holy matrimony to declare it, I realised that this appeal was addressed to me alone, and that if I neglected it now, I should be answerable to Heaven for my silence.

So, the moment the rector's voice ceased, I rose. 'I forbid the banns,' I cried. 'I know of a cause which makes this marriage unholy in the sight of God, and I am ready to declare it.'

The rector's face assumed a look of consternation that was almost ludicrous; he had only just been appointed to the living, and probably my face and identity were as yet unknown to him. For the moment he seemed at a loss what to say, and there was an audible stir and murmur among the congregation.

At length he said, 'I cannot hear you now. Come to me in the vestry after service.'

Mrs Maitland, scarlet with flurry and distress, was plucking at my cape, and I sat down quietly, and the service proceeded as usual. But I heard nothing of it, nor of the sermon that followed, for my mind was occupied with the disclosures I was pledged to make, and the effect they would produce. All too soon for me the sermon came to an end, and the congregation was dismissed; there was the scroop[12] of the benches on the pavement at the back, the breath of cooler air as the doors were opened, the clatter of the choir-boys' booths heard above the tones of the organ. All eyes were turned on me in passing, and the two churchwardens held a whispered conference with Mrs Maitland, in which I gathered they were advising her to take me away, and offering to make some explanation to the rector.

I refused to listen to her entreaties to allow her to see the rector privately first, or accompany me to the vestry, and when she saw that I was perfectly calm and determined to carry out my intention unhindered, she gave way. The church was empty now, though a few inquisitive persons still hung about the porch, and presently a little round-eyed chorister came down to tell me that the rector was ready to see me; so, leaving Mrs Maitland on a seat in the chancel, I went into the vestry alone.

Canon Broadbent, the rector, was a churchman of the suavely ecclesiastical type, portly and of goodly height and appearance; he received me with a grave courteousness, though I could see that he was displeased and anxious to get through what he evidently felt would be a painful interview.

'I will hear anything you have to tell me,' he began, 'though you must see, my dear young lady, how wrongly you have acted in disturbing the service of God and turning away the thoughts of his worshippers. Nothing but the gravest necessity can justify such conduct.'

'You called upon anyone who knew any cause against that marriage to declare it,' I said. 'How could I remain silent, knowing what I do know?'

'Reverence, common decency, should have prompted you to wait for a more convenient occasion,' he said. 'However, if you were really impelled by some overmastering sense of duty, and if the reason should prove sufficient, you may be held excusable.

But let me warn you solemnly, before you say a word of what you have come to say, of the wickedness of attempting to blast a young man's character and future by any charges which you are not fully prepared to prove. Many a man has been guilty of—of indiscretions, of which he sincerely repents later, which it would be cruel to rake up against him in order to prevent him from ever leading a clean and reputable life. Think, then, whether your motives are indeed pure and high, or whether, in accusing him, you are influenced by some mean, unworthy feeling of which you should feel heartily ashamed. And if conscience tells you that it is so, let your charge remain unspoken.'

'You are quite mistaken, Canon Broadbent,' I said. 'I bring no charge against Mr Dallas. For all I know, his past may be quite stainless—and a man's record would have to be black indeed before the Church would refuse to celebrate his marriage with the most innocent girl. But it is not a case of that here, and yet I begin to see how hard it will be to make you believe my story.'

'You cannot possibly mean to imply that Miss Heseltine——' he was beginning.

'I tell you that if you knew who and what she is who passes as Evelyn Heseltine, you would be the first to say that this marriage is too impious and blasphemous to be sanctioned by any priest.'

'These are strange words,' he said uneasily. 'I would gladly hear no more, but my duty compels me to ask you to explain them—if you can.'

'First let me ask you a question,' I said. 'Do you believe that an evil spirit may be permitted to enter into a human body?'

'Really, really,' he said, 'I cannot discuss such a subject with you—let me beg you to keep to the point, or I cannot allow you to remain here.'

'I am not wandering from the point—I am coming to it. Does not the New Testament tell us of devils being cast out of men and suffered to enter a herd of swine? Is that true, or false?'

'We must not apply too literal an interpretation to what is figurative or mystic,' he said. 'And once for all, I decline to be led into these unprofitable arguments. Do you or do you not know any reason which renders Miss Heseltine—a young lady who, from my slight acquaintance with her, seems to be endowed with every good and endearing quality—an unfit person to contract holy matrimony? And by reason—I mean such reason as the law of the land would compel me to recognise—anything less is a matter which I do not feel called upon to inquire into, which I shall refuse to listen to.'

'If the law permits a man to go through the mockery of marriage with a devil incarnate, a fiend in human shape, will the Church perform such a ceremony?' I said. 'I declare to you, Canon Broadbent, as I hope for mercy and pardon hereafter that the real Evelyn Heseltine is dead. She died in her sleep weeks ago, and the body she has put off for ever is now inhabited by a lost soul, some foul and evil spirit which has taken her form for its own vile purposes. You do not believe me, I see that, and yet the faith you hold bids you to believe that such things were not only possible but actually happened, not once but again and again, in the past. Why should you reject my story now as incredible?'

He shielded his face with his hand for a moment; when he spoke again his voice and manner were completely changed. 'My poor child,' he said, 'if I had had any idea of this I should not have spoken so harshly. I pity you from my heart. It is dreadful to think that you should be haunted by such a delusion as this. Will you try to believe me when I assure you that it is nothing more—it is simply the effect of ill-health, a disordered imagination, over-wrought nerves.'

I saw that his hand was shaking and his mouth twitching, that he avoided looking me in the face.

'I am not ill,' I said. 'I am as well as I could hope to be under such persecution as I have had to bear, day after day, night after night. And my mind is as clear as yours, Canon Broadbent. I think my nerves are the steadier just now. I did not come to you for pity. I want help, counsel; have you none to give me?'

'I can only pray for you,' he said, 'pray that God may see fit to remove this cloud from you. But you yourself must do something, too, to prevent these ideas from preying upon you. Lead as active a life as you can, try to take up some pursuit—work, play, anything but brood—and by-and-by, very soon, I trust, the sunshine will come back. You will recover your mental tone and see how morbid and imaginary the terror is that now seems so real and vivid.'

'All words,' I said, 'empty phrases. Do you really suppose they can help or comfort me? I loved the Evelyn Heseltine that was —loved her dearly, little as I did to show it. Is it likely that I should imagine or invent this hideous thing about her, or that I should loathe and dread her as I do unless I had been given the strongest cause? I *know* that I am under no mistake, and in your heart, Canon Broadbent, you know it too. You *do* believe my story, only you dare not admit it, for fear of the consequences. You clergymen are cowards after all. When you come upon the devil you profess to fight, you prefer to turn aside and let him go his way unhindered!'

He did not attempt to answer me, but opened the door that led into the chancel and called to Mrs Maitland.

'I think,' he said to her, 'you had better take your friend home at once, and if you have not already called in medical advice, it might be advisable, if this mental agitation does not pass off soon. Poor young creature, she is greatly to be pitied!'

He had lowered his voice, but I heard every word distinctly.

'I am indeed to be pitied,' I said, 'when the priest who represents Heaven here, delivers me over to the powers of Hell.'

My shaft went home, I know, but he merely bowed his head without reply, as he accompanied us down the nave and through the churchyard to the gate, where our carriage was waiting for us; and Mrs Maitland and I drove back through the deep dusty lanes in silence, for both of us, I daresay, felt that any speech was dangerous just then.

Evelyn met us as we entered the house. 'How late you are!' she cried. 'What can have kept you so long?' I looked her full in the face, and I saw by her eyes that she knew, or at least guessed, that I had made one more attempt to defy and thwart her.

'We are late,' I replied calmly, 'because I forbade your banns and I had to explain my reasons to Canon Broadbent afterwards in the vestry.'

She started, as if my courage took her by surprise, as probably it did. 'I don't understand,' she said innocently. 'Oh, Stella, what have you done? I can't believe it—you *couldn't* have done this!'

'Ask Mrs Maitland,' I said as I passed up the staircase, and before I reached my room I heard Evelyn's low weeping. What could I do against such black hypocrisy? How could I hope to overthrow an adversary who had all the forces of the world, the flesh and the devil at her disposal?

I did not go down again all that day, and for many days afterwards I kept my room. The reaction after the scene I had gone through, the sense of utter failure and defeat, and the dread of the consequences proved too much for my strength. The doctor came and talked oracular platitudes about nervous breakdown and the necessity of absolute quiet and freedom from excitement or worry, until I could have screamed with rage at his bland incompetence. But even he did not venture to pronounce me mad, for Canon Broadbent had been discreetly silent about the denunciation I had made in the vestry, and my action in forbidding the banns was no doubt accounted for by some private jealousy.

I knew that consultations and discussions were going on, and that some pressure had been put upon Evelyn to send me home to my family or have me placed in a home where I should be under supervision, though I gathered that she had insisted on my remaining at Tansted for the present.

She was more perfidiously affectionate and attentive than ever; she paid me frequent visits during the day, and studiously avoided any allusion to my outbreak, while my nights were no longer made a misery to me by her secret persecution. I almost began to think that she had relented at last, seeing how completely she had triumphed and how feeble and powerless I had now become, but I deceived myself.

This clemency of hers was only apparent. She knew that I was not strong enough as yet to feel the full effect of her devilish tortures, and she did not intend to lose her victim until she had forced me to witness her final triumph.

On the night before her wedding-day she came to me once more in her bridal attire, so lovely a vision that I was dazzled by her unearthly beauty, but the eyes that gleamed through the transparent veil were as baleful and malignant as of old, and the soft lips dropped an even deadlier venom than before into my poor tortured brain.

For she talked of Hugh; as he was now—self-respecting, wholesome-minded, unsuspicious, hopeful of a long and happy married life with a companion who was his ideal of goodness and loveliness; and what he would become through her—disillusioned, perverted, degraded, loathing his bondage and yet unable to resist her power over his senses, acquiescing sullenly and cynically in his own shame and disgrace. She hated him now, she said, because he had loved me first, and might perhaps come to love me again. But I should never profit by it; after to-morrow he would be hers, and in a very short time I should be a prisoner within the impassable walls of an asylum, with lunatics and idiots for my only companions, and love, happiness, hope shut out of my life for ever. She told me how she would bring Hugh to see me, the wreck of my former self, my mind shattered, my beauty perished, and how he should learn that it was love of him that had made me thus. And she reminded me that I had brought my misery on myself; that if I had only restrained my groundless, morbid jealousy of the girl who was dead, if I had only interfered when there was yet time to prevent her from taking that drug, all would have been different. Instead of the wretched, unloved, conscience-stricken woman I was now, I should be lying peacefully asleep, or waiting in happy wakefulness for the morning to break which would bring my wedding-day.

There was more than this, which I dare not repeat, and nothing I could say would give any impression of the awful wickedness, the ingenuity of cruel invention and suggestion which made these taunts so appalling. I cannot believe that even the guiltiest sinners in hell can be subjected to worse mental torment than she forced me to endure that night. It was terrible to feel that I was the object of such a deliberate and intense hatred.

At last even her malignity exhausted itself for the time, but long after she had left me I lay tossing and writhing under the sting of those poisoned whispers, until it faded out in merciful sleep, and the dream which came to me was not frightful, but tender and pathetic.

I thought that Evelyn—the real Evelyn who was now in Heaven—came and sorrowed over me and comforted me, assuring me that she understood and forgave me, and would willingly help me if she were allowed. I thought she told me not to despair, that evil would not triumph for ever, or perhaps for long, that my term of punishment was drawing to an end.

And I woke crying for joy with the touch of her hair upon my cheeks and the pressure of her loving arm about my neck, and though I knew it was nothing but a dream, it left me strangely strengthened and consoled.

That morning was to see Hugh's marriage, and yet my heart was lighter than it had been for many a day. I found myself hoping once more.

As the hours passed I heard the bustle of preparation, and knew that Evelyn was being made ready for the ceremony, that she would soon follow her bridesmaids to the church. I believe she actually came in to see me before she left, but I feigned to be asleep, and she went away softly.

Gradually the house became still; most of the servants had probably gone to see their young mistress married; the nurse who attended on me had gone downstairs after locking my door, as if she thought I was likely to make my escape.

It began to strike me that it was a considerable time since I had heard the carriage drive away. Surely before this the wedding bells ought to have pealed out—if nothing had happened to interrupt the marriage.

And all at once I understood what this hope was that had come to me so unaccountably. I knew that it was not without some basis.

There were things that even devils dare not do. I remembered that Evelyn had not attended church for some weeks—not, I was almost sure, since the change. Would she venture now to cross the threshold of God's house? If not, her terror must betray her as an unholy being, even to the most incredulous. The rector would remember my warning; her spells would be broken.

The church was not so far away but that the bells, when rung, could be distinctly heard across the fields. I went to the window and leaned out, holding my breath and straining my ears in the direction from which the sound should come. I heard nothing but the whirr and click of the reaping machine amongst the corn, the calling of birds, and the lowing of cattle.

I waited until I could doubt no longer. Something *had* prevented this monstrous marriage. I fell on my knees and thanked God fervently, entreating His pardon for having supposed that He would suffer His temple to be so desecrated.

And, as I rose, there was borne on the breeze, faint but unmistakable, the ripple and clash of wedding bells.

They were married. She had entered God's house, knelt before His altar, and He had not interposed. Perhaps there was no God, and if there were, it mattered little, for the Devil was master in this miserable world!

The last thing I was conscious of that day was the clang of those triumphant, derisive bells, which seemed to be battering my brains into a throbbing pulp.

IX

There was an interval after that as to which my memory is almost a blank. I can only just recall a long confused nightmare, through which I was making the most superhuman efforts to prevent Hugh's marriage, pursuing him and Evelyn to the furthest ends of the earth, always on the verge of overtaking them, always hindered by every conceivable obstacle and delay, trying to rouse everyone I met to see Hugh's danger and help me to avert it, and telling my story over and over again, and then, just as I seemed to have succeeded, hearing those dreadful bells which told me that it was too late.

This must have gone on for some weeks, for when the fever left me, and I was once more able to notice the common things around me, I saw that the roses that I had last seen climbing round my casement had turned to scarlet pods, and the buds were too shrivelled and nipped to unfold themselves. From my window I looked out upon a late autumn landscape of russet and orange, and the lawn was littered with fallen leaves, and the paths white with hoar-frost.

I knew I must have had a long illness but I was too weak and my mind too sluggish as yet to make any effort to remember what had brought it on. I was content for the time to lead a sort of

animal existence, and to find a negative comfort and even enjoyment in the little luxuries, the trivial incidents of convalescence.

And then, when it all came back—Evelyn's death and strange
resuscitation, her treachery and malignity, and the arts by which
she had beguiled my lover from me—it seemed too fantastic, too
unreal to be anything but the perverted imaginings of delirium.

I knew that Hugh and Evelyn were married, but I no longer
cared. My passion for Hugh seemed to have burnt itself out; even
my terror of Evelyn had left me, or so at least I persuaded myself.

As I grew stronger I asked for news of them, and found that
they had already returned from their wedding journey and were
now at Laleham Court.

It seemed to me a little strange that Evelyn had not yet come
over to see me, and I said as much to Mrs Maitland, and told her
how I was longing to see her again. This was quite true, for I
was anxious to be quite sure that my hallucinations were indeed
cured, and I could not be that until I met Evelyn.

Mrs Maitland put me off with palpable excuses. It was better
that I should not see Evelyn just yet, until I was perfectly strong
and well again.

'I am almost well now,' I said. 'I am quite able to see her, if she
cared enough about me to come.'

To this Mrs Maitland replied that Evelyn herself had not been
strong enough to go out at all of late.

'Then let me go and see her,' I pleaded.

'Hugh thinks that you had better not meet just yet,' she said.
'He is quite distressed about the change in her—it is making him
absolutely miserable.'

'You are keeping something from me,' I said suddenly. 'Don't
you see that, unless you want me to be ill again, you had better
be quite frank. I have had ideas, strange, horrible fancies, about
Evelyn, and they will never quite leave me until I see her again.'

'My dear,' she said, 'I think I can guess, from certain things you
talked of in your delirium, what those ideas are. You seemed to
be under the delusion that you had given Evelyn chloral on some
occasion, and that she had died of it. Surely you know now that it
was all a dream—that nothing of the sort ever happened.'

'Isn't it true, then, that you came downstairs that evening last

June and asked me if you might give Evelyn a few drops of the chloral you knew I had, and whether it would do her any harm, and that I said it would not. Did I imagine that?'

'No, my dear, that is all true. I thought she seemed excited and wanted something to make her sleep.'

'God help me!' I cried, 'you have brought it all back. I knew that chloral was dangerous to anyone with a weak heart; I had read it in some medical book, and I let you give it to her, and—ah, I remember now!'

'You poor thing! and you have been allowing this to prey on you when, if I had only known, I could have relieved your mind at once. Why, my dear, you have nothing to accuse yourself of. The fact is, I never gave Evelyn any chloral at all. When I went into her room she was already dozing, and I waited until she had fallen into a good sound sleep, and then I put out the lights, and came away without even opening the bottle. Luckily, I believe I can prove it.' She went out and presently returned with a small fluted phial. 'See, here is the very bottle, with the cover still round the stopper just as it left the chemist. Now, my dear, I hope you realise that you have been tormenting yourself for nothing at all?'

'If only I had known this at the time!' I cried. 'Oh, why—why didn't you tell me?'

'Well, Evelyn told you that morning that the bottle was in my keeping, and afterwards she expressly warned me not to mention the subject again in case you might ask me to give it back to you. We both hoped you had forgotten all about it. Of course, dear Evelyn had no more idea than I had that you were brooding over it like this, or we should have put it right at once.'

The good, simple-minded lady was under the impression that she had set my mind entirely at rest, whereas she had only succeeded in convincing me that the thing which I was again beginning to consider a delusion was an awful reality.

What did it signify that the chloral had not been administered? It was none the less true that I had found Evelyn dead the next morning, that in my madness I had invoked some hellish spirit to save me from the consequences of my supposed guilt.

I saw now how I had been tricked and betrayed from the first, how the cunning fiend had used my confession against me, compelling me, in self-protection, to serve her wicked purpose. Perhaps, even if I had known the truth then, and refused to acknowledge her at the first, the result would have been the same, but at least I should have been spared the load of needless guilt and shame, the humiliation of feeling myself indebted to such protection as hers.

Ah! how I hated this merciless devil for all the wanton, unnecessary suffering she had made me endure, and how it maddened me to think of what Hugh Dallas must be going through by this time! If I had been eager to see them before, judge how intensely I desired it now, how I burned to discover for myself how far she had revealed her true nature to him, and how he had been affected by so terrible a disenchantment.

But I have considerable power of self-control when I choose to exercise it, and I knew how necessary it was for his sake to disguise my anxiety. I managed to make Mrs Maitland believe that I had entirely thrown off what she would have considered my 'delusion.' Outwardly I was quite calm, and I was soon allowed to come downstairs and resume my share in the quiet, everyday routine of the house, working and reading and walking with Mrs Maitland as I had once done with Evelyn.

I discovered that she and Hugh were living at Laleham Court in the strictest seclusion; no callers had succeeded in seeing her since her return; it was understood that her health was not strong enough to allow her to accept invitations, and he himself was said to be too much concerned about his wife to leave her, except when absolutely compelled by his duties.

To me all this was full of sinister significance, and only heightened the suspense in which I lived; but I bided my time, feeling certain that, sooner or later, Hugh and I would meet, and the first glance at his face would tell me all I longed to know.

And one afternoon I was told that he was in the drawing-room and wished to see me, and though my heart leapt wildly at the news, and my head swam at the thought that I was really to see him at last, really to have an answer to the fear that gave me no rest, I went in and met him with perfect self-possession.

How woefully he had changed; there was a grey pallor on his face that made him look prematurely old and haggard, his eyes had an expression of suppressed despair, his manner was rest-less and nervous—it was only too plain that already the iron had entered into his soul, and that, if possible, he was as wretched as I!

And yet, stricken and changed as he was, the sight of him revived the old mad passion which I thought was dead. I loved him more intensely and devotedly than ever—I would have died for him willingly if my death could give him back all this fiend had robbed him of!

The beginning of our conversation was commonplace and conventional enough. He said he was glad to find that I had so completely recovered from my illness; I replied that I was per-fectly well now, but was sorry to hear such unfavourable accounts of Evelyn.

I watched his face narrowly as I spoke, and saw a spasm come across it at her name.

'I am unhappy about her,' he said, 'more unhappy and anxious every day. I can hardly speak of it.'

'Do you think I don't know how terribly you are suffering?' I said gently. 'Do you think I don't feel for you?'

'God knows it is hard!' he said with a half groan, 'when I look back on what she was, and what I hoped she would be, and know what I can't help knowing, struggle against it as I may. And I am so helpless, so utterly powerless to keep this misery from coming upon me! I can only wait, and feel there is no hope. She talks sometimes as if we were to be together for many years to come, and it is almost more than I can bear. The irony of it all! But I didn't mean to speak of all this. I—I have a message to you—from her. She is very anxious to see you again. I—I had to promise I would tell you, and bring you back with me, if you feel able to come.'

What new device, I wondered, had she invented to torture me? I could see that he only delivered the message with the great-est reluctance, as if he would have spared me if it had been in his power. 'I will gladly come,' I said, 'if you wish it, if you think I can be of use to you.'

'I did my best to dissuade her,' he said. 'I was afraid of the con-sequences if I let you see her just now. But she has so set her heart on seeing you that I dared not risk refusing her. And now I have seen you, I can't think there is any danger. Only, you must promise me that you will say nothing to—to disturb her—above all, you must not let her know that I have spoken to you like this. Can I trust you? Are you quite sure that you can depend on yourself?'

His voice shook with an anxiety he dared not confess in words. I knew well that it was not for himself he feared, and it touched me more than I can say to feel that he could think of me just then.

'You need not be afraid on my account,' I said. 'I can't explain it, but I feel as if, in some way I don't understand at present, I shall be able to help you by this meeting—perhaps even free you from this awful shadow that is darkening your life.'

'It is too late for that,' he said sadly. 'When you see her you will understand what little hope there is for me. Can you come with me now? I have the phaeton[13] here, and it need not take you very long to get ready.'

In a few minutes more we were in the carriage together on our way to Laleham. Neither of us spoke much, or except on ordinary topics; it seemed as if we both shunned, by common consent, any further reference to the subject that was really engrossing our thoughts.

But to me there was an exquisite, pathetic happiness in being with him, and knowing that, though he could not tell me so in words, he understood me now as he had never done before, that we were drawn to one another by the fellowship of secret suffering. And all the way I was racking my brain to find some means of delivering him. I felt prepared to run any risk, make any sacrifice, if only I could induce the evil spirit to give up her prey; and yet what arguments, or threats or prayers, that I could use would have any effect upon her? I saw how unlikely it was that I could prevail against such an antagonist, but nevertheless I looked forward to the contest without fear, with even a strong hope that I might be enabled to find some vulnerable place in her armour.

Hugh drove fast, and it was still quite light when we entered the gates of a park and reached the stately Elizabethan house which was Laleham Court.

As soon as we were inside, he led the way up a wide staircase and along a corridor to Evelyn's sitting-room.

She was lying on a couch near the fire, and the face she turned to us as we entered told its own tale. All the softness and girlishness had gone from it; there were circles round the eyes, which glittered with a strange brilliance; her cheeks were sharpened in outline and sunken, the mouth had a hard, drawn look. It was terrible to see how soon the evil soul had set its impress on the features that had once been so fair.

She had not lost her old malicious pleasure in torturing me by mock endearments. 'Dearest Stella,' she began, 'I have thought of you so often and longed to come over and see you—but they would not let me. So, as soon as I heard from Aunt Lucy that you were quite well again, I insisted on Hugh's bringing you here. I have been ill myself, as I daresay you know, but I am ever so much better now—only rather weak still. I really believe poor Hugh fancied he was going to lose me at one time, but I tell him I am not so easily got rid of. I am much too fond of Laleham—and perhaps a little of him too—to bear to give it all up just yet. I mean to live for years and years to come.'

I glanced at Hugh, whose face she could not see, and the agony I read there wrung my heart.

'I am glad you sent for me,' I said quietly. 'I have been wishing to see you too for a long time. We have a great deal to say to one another.'

'Yes,' she said, 'a great deal. Hugh, you won't mind leaving Stella with me for half an hour, will you? It is so long since we have had a real talk!'

'I think,' he said slowly, 'I had better stay and see that you don't tire yourself.'

'What nonsense!' she exclaimed, with a touch of anger. 'I am not an invalid now, and it won't tire me to talk to Stella.'

'Then,' he said, with a forced playfulness, 'I will stay to protect Miss Maberly—she has been ill, too, remember.'

'Can't you see that you are not wanted!' she said. 'Hugh, how dense you are getting! I insist on your leaving us to our two selves at once. I tell you I wish it—and you know how dangerous it is to refuse me anything I have particularly set my heart on!'

'Go,' I whispered, as he still seemed to hesitate, 'you will only do harm by opposing her. You need not be afraid to leave me here.'

'You will not forget my warning?' he replied in an undertone, 'you will be careful, will you not?'

'You may trust me,' I said. 'I am not the weak, unstrung creature I used to be.'

'I daren't thwart her now,' he said, half to himself; 'and, after all, what possible danger—?' He went up to Evelyn and kissed her, which I knew he would not have done but for his anxiety on my account. 'There,' he said, 'you shall have your own way. I'll leave you for a little while, but remember I shall be within call, if you want me.'

This last sentence, as I perfectly understood, was really meant for my ear. He obviously suspected that she had some evil object to gratify, and wished me to feel that help was at hand.

'He thinks I can't possibly get on long without him!' she exclaimed, with a mocking little laugh, 'but I knew Stella before I knew you, my dear Hugh, so you mustn't be too conceited, and now go down to your own den, and don't come back until you are sent for.'

He looked searchingly at me once more, and then, seeing that I remained quite calm and mistress of myself, he went, though I fancied that he still had misgivings.

There was no need, for I felt absolutely unafraid, as if in some way the spell that Evelyn had exercised over me all those wretched weeks had been broken.

As soon as he had gone I turned to Evelyn and fixed my eyes steadily on her face.

'I am wondering what you want with me now,' I said quietly. 'What made you send him to fetch me like this?'

'What reason could I have?' was the smooth, false answer, 'except that I was longing to see you again, dearest Stella, and satisfy myself that you were quite strong and well again?'

'Yes, I am strong now,' I said. 'You cannot torment me any longer as you used to do. I know at last—what you cunningly kept from me—that I never was the murderess by proxy you taunted me with being—that the chloral was never given.'

She started. 'The chloral? why, of course it was not,' she cried. 'Oh, Stella, can't you forget all those dreadful ideas? Don't you understand how incapable I am of tormenting or taunting you now? I am sure you wouldn't wish to distress me by talking like this, when you see that I am not quite strong enough to bear it yet!'

'You are trying to delude me again, to put me off my guard —but you will not,' I said. 'I am not to be deceived, even though you look like a woman who is dying fast. I know very well you will not die yet.'

'Die!' she repeated with a shudder. 'Oh, no, no. I *can't* die now—not so soon. I *won't* die. Life is so beautiful. I couldn't leave Hugh!'

'Do you mean,' I said, 'that you love him—*you!*'

'Do I love him? Better and better every day I live!'

'You did not love him when you bewitched him into caring for you. You meant to drag him down to your level, and delight in his degradation. Now you have discovered that, though you may break his heart, blacken and befoul all that he held fair, you cannot debase *him*—his nature is too high for that. And so you have ended by loving him, when his own love is dead, changed to loathing and hate. Yes, you have been caught in your own devilish snare. The life you snatched at so greedily has become a worse hell than that you escaped from. There *is* a God after all, and He is punishing you here in the world where you have no right!'

'Stella!' she cried, trembling, 'I cannot let you say these violent things to me—they are horrible and untrue. Please, please go away if you can't be kind and gentle. You are making me ill. Have you no pity?'

'What pity had you on me?' I said. 'You came between Hugh and me, you took him away from me, did your best to wreck his life and mine. If it is in my power now to make you suffer in your turn, why should I spare you?'

There was a small mirror lying on a table close by, and I took it up and held it before her. 'Look in this,' I said. 'Is that the face that bewitched Hugh? The face is what the soul makes of it, and even in this short time yours has begun to betray you. You boasted that your beauty would keep him your slave in spite of all he knew, and see, even your beauty is changing, passing, perishing. Soon the terrible signs he has learnt to read in those lines and hollows will be written more plainly still, so that none can mistake their meaning. Will that be better than death itself?'

She pushed the mirror away with a passionate gesture. 'I don't want to look,' she cried. 'I know I am altered, but I am not going to die, and Hugh loves me, he *does*, whatever you may say. Why should I care? Only that *you* should be so cruel to me, Stella, just when I thought—it is that that almost breaks my heart!'

Her grief was so naturally feigned that for the moment I myself felt a prick of shame and compunction, as though it were some tender innocent creature that I had been hurting, and not a corrupt and subtle spirit, baffled and in desperate straits, but still capable of evil.

'If I seem cruel,' I said, 'I have a motive. I want to make you see how worthless this life is you cling to so desperately, that, though you may not die, your life will only become a greater burden and misery every day you live. If you really and sincerely loved Hugh, you would prove it by setting him free. Who knows that, if you voluntarily quit this frame and return to your former state, there may not be mercy and pardon for you, even now? What possible attraction can there be in such life as yours?'

'Life is sweet,' she replied. 'I may never be what I was, I may not have long to be here, but I want to live as long as possible.'

At the words a sudden idea came into my mind. I saw at last a means of saving Hugh. 'You wish to live?' I said. 'Suppose you were offered not only life, but health, strength, the beauty you value so much, on one condition—would you accept it? Listen to me. I love Hugh, as you know, but I am willing never to see him again, to forfeit all hope of happiness here, and, for all I know, hereafter, if only I can feel that I have freed him from you for ever. You say you love him—but it is life you really love, you dread going back to what you were. This is my proposal. To-night, before the clock has struck twelve, I promise that I will find some means of passing out of this body for ever, leaving it for you to enter, provided that you undertake to abandon your present form and never seek to entangle Hugh in any way whatever. Do you agree?'

She gave a sort of hysterical sob. 'Stella,' she cried, 'you can't be in earnest, surely you know that what you are saying is sheer madness?'

'Oh, I am not mad,' I said. 'You used to threaten to drive me into an asylum—but you could not. I am perfectly reasonable, I am not proposing anything that is impossible. If you were able to re-animate one dead body, you can surely take possession of mine after I have left it. And it is young and strong; it will live for years, you will gain by such an exchange. Once more I ask you —do you accept my terms?'

She looked wildly all round her, panting like a thing at bay. 'What am I to say?' she cried. 'Yes, yes, I accept—I agree to any- thing—anything!'

'Will you swear to me, by the Power you serve, that you will abandon this body to-night, and that, as Stella Maberly, you will trouble Hugh no more?'

'Have I not said so?' she asked hoarsely. 'Now you are satisfied —leave me.'

Something in her manner excited my suspicions. 'How can I be sure that you are not tricking me?' I said. 'Perhaps even this illness of yours is only some cunning device. What if I kept my part of the compact and you broke yours and lived on, to torture Hugh and mock at me for being fool enough to imagine any oath had power to bind you? I believe you mean treachery—I see it in your eyes!'

'Oh, no, no!' she cried, wringing her hands. 'Indeed, indeed I am not treacherous. Don't frighten me any more, Stella, only go now!'

It occurred to me that there was an easy way of putting her to the test. 'Why should we wait?' I said. 'Why should we not both kill ourselves—here—now?'

'Not yet,' she said, 'how can we? We have no—no weapons.'

'Did I not see some Oriental swords and daggers on the wall in the corridor outside as I came here?' I asked.

'Yes,' she cried. 'You will find them at the end of the passage. Bring two, or—I know where they are—let me go and fetch them.'

I laughed. 'Liar!' I said, 'there are no weapons hanging there. I said it to try you. I know what was in your mind; you would have locked yourself in here, or rushed downstairs and given the alarm.'

She sank into a seat, trembling. 'It doesn't matter,' I said. 'I know what I wanted to know. I have changed my mind. My plan that we should both commit suicide was absurd—I see that now. I give it up.'

Her face relaxed. 'I was sure you would see how impossible it was,' she said faintly and with difficulty.

'I do see it,' I agreed. 'You would never have killed yourself; you refuse to release Hugh, you mean to go on torturing and maddening him as you tortured me for years. But you shall not. When I came here I thought that, being a fiend in human form, you could not be killed. But if that was so you would not be afraid of me—and you are, you are! So I am going to try. Call for help if you like—it will be useless. Both these doors are bolted and locked, and I have the keys.'

She opened her dry lips as if to scream for help, but her voice seemed paralysed by fear, for no sound came from them as she crouched there, with her great eyes fixed on me and her hands pressed close against her heart. Suddenly she made a spring towards the bell-rope, but I was too quick for her. Before she could reach it I seized her slender neck with both my hands and forced her back upon the couch, gripping her throat with all my might—harder, harder, and harder still, until she ceased to resist.

Up to that moment I had not been certain that any force of mine could drive this devil forth against her will, and half expected that she would escape and mock me after all, but I felt armed with irresistible strength just then, and soon, sooner than I expected, the thing was done.

As I relinquished my hold and the form sank down in a huddled heap among the cushions, I had a vision of a shape, with a wicked, beautiful face, that was not Evelyn's, distorted with impotent rage and terror and despair, which stood there in the waning light and seemed to be striving to revenge itself upon me before it fled to its doom, and I own that for one dreadful instant I was in deadly fear.

And then, just as I gave myself up for lost, the shape appeared to quiver and melt away into nothingness, and I was alone with Evelyn's dead body.

I raised it gently and arranged the cushions under the head, so that she lay as if asleep, exactly as she had lain that summer morning; the face was calm and pure and sweet once more, the very face of the girl I loved. 'Do you understand?' I whispered, as I bent over her and kissed her softly on the forehead. 'The evil thing has left you for ever, you poor, innocent clay. Sleep in peace, for you are all Evelyn's now!'

Then I went out, and half way down the corridor I met Hugh.

He seemed glad to see me safe and unharmed. 'I was just coming up to carry you away,' he said. 'I was getting anxious, but I might have known I could trust you. There is nothing wrong?' he added; 'she—she is not worse?'

'No, no,' I said. 'She is well, quite well now. Hugh, dear, dear Hugh, all this long misery is over for you and for me! I was determined to free you from the horror that has been hanging over you if I could—and God has helped me, Hugh; it is gone—gone for ever!'

He could not believe it at first. 'Gone!' he cried. 'What do you mean?'

'Go to her,' I said gently, 'and you will understand.'

I saw him rush to the door of her room and go in, and then, feeling that he must be left to himself just then, I went down the staircase and into a big hall which seemed to be used as a morning-room.

I could not rest, I paced up and down in a kind of mystical exaltation; the old portraits in ruff and doublet looked down on me with grim approval from the walls, the armorial shields in the oriel window glowed like blood in the last gleams of the sunset. I heard bells being rung furiously, hurrying footsteps, cries and commotion, but no one came near me, and though I still felt no remorse and knew that I had only done what was just and righteous, I began by degrees to be afraid of the solitude there in the slowly darkening hall.

I wanted to see Hugh, to hear him thanking me for his deliverance, vowing to prove me guiltless in the eyes of all the world, to stand by me to the last. When once I had seen that in his face, as I did not doubt I should, the others might condemn me as a murderess, imprison me, take my life, and I should not care—I should have had my reward.

At last I could not bear to be alone any longer; I felt I must go to Hugh. The old house had settled down into a dead stillness that yet was not quiet—only a breathless waiting for something that was about to happen.

I passed into the entrance hall and met a footman coming down one of the passages with a lighted lamp. He started as he saw me, his face went white, and he nearly dropped the lamp for terror; he had not been at the door when I arrived, and probably imagined that I was a ghost.

'Where is your master?' I said. 'I am Miss Maberly, and I wish to see him.'

'Mr Dallas is in the library, miss,' he answered; 'but he doesn't wish to be disturbed just now. I was bringing in this lamp, but he told me to take it away and leave him alone.'

'He will see *me*,' I said; 'show me where the library is.'

He put down a lamp and led the way to a door, which he tried to open. 'It's been locked since I went in,' he said. 'Perhaps you haven't heard that there's trouble in the house, miss,' he added in a lowered voice.

'I know,' I replied. 'But Mr Dallas will open the door to me. That will do, you can go.'

I knocked softly at the door. 'Hugh,' I said, 'I am here—Stella —won't you let me in?'

And there was silence for a moment, though I thought I heard him moving as if to open the door, and then a terrible sound rang out within the closed room—the report of a pistol—and I knew that my sacrifice had been in vain.

Here this statement shall end. I have had much to undergo since; indignities of every kind, confinement, long and purpose-less examinations, odious charges and misconstructions, and then the mockery of mercy which consigned me to the place where I am now, and where I suppose I shall remain till death releases me.

But why should I write of it all? Nothing seems worth resenting, telling, remembering even, that followed the terrible moment when I realised that Hugh had deserted me, leaving me to bear my penalty alone.

What led him to do so—in the very hour of regaining his freedom, and when he must have known that he was the one person whose evidence could have placed my conduct in its true light—I do not understand. I never shall understand here.

But I have never blamed *him;* I feel certain that he could never have been a coward, or intentionally disloyal and ungrateful to the woman who had risked everything for his sake. It is far more probable that the evil spirit which hated me contrived to avenge her defeat by some last effort of devilish malignity.

And, whatever the explanation may be, I know that Hugh will make it all clear to me himself some day, when we are re-united and nothing wicked and malevolent can come near us any more.

And so I am seldom absolutely unhappy, even in the daytime; while the night no longer brings terror with it—but only consolation and peace.

For although, whenever I dream at all, I am back at Tansted once more, somehow it is always those days of early June that I live over again in the old garden and house; the Evelyn whom I find there is my dearest friend, and the perfect sweetness of our intercourse is never marred by any haunting half-consciousness of misery and horror to come.

This is a mercy which I know I do not deserve, and for which I trust I am not ungrateful, and yet I long impatiently for the day when all suspense and uncertainty and bewilderment will end, and I shall rest and understand—for I am very weary of waiting.

THE END

NOTES

1   *'come out'*: Stella's 'coming-out' is her formal entrance into society. Most of her "well-born and well-to-do" schoolfellows would also have been débutantes.

2   *whip-lash fountain*: non-standard term for what is presumably quite an elaborate fountain, with revolving jets

3   *chloral*: Chloral hydrate was a common nineteenth-century treatment for insomnia and anxiety.

4   *wrapper*: a sleeved apron tied at the back

5   *bromide or sulphonal*: These drugs are sedatives and hypnotics, and would also commonly treat nervous complaints.

6   *dog-cart*: So called not because it was drawn by dogs but because its special feature was a box for transporting them, this is an open riding carriage.

7   *'Qui veut la fin veut les moyens'*: proverbial, the desire for the end implies a desire for the means

8   *in ordinary*: obsolete expression meaning "ordinarily"

9   *proosic acid*: The use of prussic acid in animal euthanasia was standard at the time to which Stella is looking back. Battersea Dogs' Home then led the way with the introduction, from 1884, of a more humane alternative. See Garry Jenkins, *A Home of Their Own: The Heart-Warming 150-Year History of Battersea Dogs and Cats Home* (2010; repr., London: Bantam Press, 2011), 116-117.

10   *moue*: This is a pout, in its faintest and most fetching form. In Chapter 11 of *Vice Versâ* Anstey refers to "that slight contortion of the features, which with a pretty girl is euphemised as a 'moue,' and with a plain one is called 'making a face.'"

11   *Blenheim*: The Blenheim variety of spaniel is white with chestnut markings.

12   *scroop*: onomatopoeic equivalent of "scrape"

13   *phaeton*: "a species of four-wheeled open carriage, ... usually driven by a pair of horses" (*Oxford English Dictionary*)

APPENDIX I

The Statement of V.M.

[127v]

The Statement of V.M. patient at Bethnal House Asylum, July: 19: 1886

This narrative is intended to be read by Mrs Morgan, Matron, Dr Miller & Dr Will.

A detailed account of the difficulties & misery that I had to contend with during the time that I was so troubled by the hearing of what I then & now believe were the voices at least some of dear relatives whom I knew were dead.

Voices & Shadows or
Mental Struggles

Hearing voices when no living creature is near is generally called a delusion. In other words they are considered insane. But when it comes to not only hearing but actually seeing the forms from which sounds proceeded little doubt 'something was wrong' a fact which I discovered in a very extraordinary manner.

Long felt lowspirited—presentiment that something awful was about to happen. Sleepless. I & my husband then in apartments at house of an unmarried M.R.C.S.[1] A lady had the drawing room floor with the floor above.

I returned home one night from a Temperance Lodge meeting[2] at about 10.30. Found a beautiful bright light burning in hall & a lady with long hair reaching down to her waist ascending stairs. I thought it was the housekeeper's sister. I followed her.

She passed to the rooms above mine, then used as lumber rooms. No sound or rustle. I heard whispering on landing. As I entered my room it seemed as if the owners of the voices entered with me. I spoke to Housekeeper who said I imagined it all & to my husband who laughed. I slept alone as my restlessness disturbed him. I lay on the sofa in the sitting-room.

[127r]

It was not a human beign. [*sic*] Going downstairs backwards. The chest on the landing—the idea that it contained the mystery.

[126v]

As night advanced & street noises ceaced (*sic*) I thought what an awful misfortune it would be were Mind & Body both to give way again. I had been ill once some years before. So I came to the conclusion that I would keep myself as quiet as possible & say very little about my condition.

Reading-sofa drawn to table when I became aware that some-one was standing close beside me—faint sigh—low murmur-ing—no one there—I went to tell my husband but he spoke so unkindly to me that I returned but not to rest.

Suddenly I heard as if there was water dropping from ceiling on to carpet—like very large drops falling at intervals with a thud. Went to part where sound proceeded but strangely enough the sound seemed to come from an opposite direction—the whispers now ceaced [*sic*]—I thought I was really going mad—low knock at the door—no one there.

Saw the long-haired lady pass window on upper landing. Now was my time to solve this mystery. I was not the least afraid in fact I felt angry—went upstairs—no one there.

How can I describe the horror of my situation. Let anyone who reads this imagine themselves in my place & ask themselves what they would have done. Under the circumstances a woman would in all probability faint—a man would use some bad lan-guage, perhaps call himself a fool. I did neither.

Prostrated by hours of Torture & Annoyance. It slowly

dawned upon me that I must be haunted. Either hopelessly helplessly mad or my vision impaired.

Next day about noon. Carriage drew up at door—the Doctor
went out hurriedly—a dark foreign looking gentleman came in
& went up to drawing room where he talked with Doctor. Then
the Doctor he and the lady who had the drawing room drove off
together.

Housekeeper (also a midwife) also left the house judging from
her dress. Likely to remain away some time.

[125v]

The manservant was also away at another of the Doctor's
homes. Only one servant left in lower part of house. Now was
my time to get some laudanum. In the Surgery—the large closet
with 10 bottles, sticks & skulls. Return of Doctor. I got in closet,
locked door, & had good view of room through keyhole. The
Doctor & the husband brought in lady & put her on sofa—
removed her bonnet & shawl. Husband refused to let her go to
her room till she had had a strengthening draught. The others
conversed apart.

I shall now leave them conversing for a while & proceed to
give you a glimpse of the nightside of this Doctor's nature.

He was one of those men who would not shrink from lending
himself to anything dishonourable & mean provided that 1st his
pocket was well filled with gold 2^{ndly} that his name was shielded
against suspicion. But like the old saying If you touch pitch you
must put up with the consequences so it was with this gentleman.
His name was very often associated with deeds of evil & I fully
believe with truth. He had a hairbreadth escape once for having
given his signature to a forged will, also with wrongly certifying
as to the cause of death & also with having illegally practised on
females an act punishable by law.[3] I have even heard respectable
people say they heard that Dr. T— buried some of his victims in
his underground cellar.

I heard them conversing—glancing through bundle of
papers—both attempted to persuade the lady to drink the mixture. She refused & accused husband of trying to poison her—
also of spending her money badly & wishing to kill her & get the
remainder.

It struck me as being strange that they should insist. Matters brought to climax—Doctor went in search of something—returning they both poured the mixture down her throat. What a dreadful scene. How she tried to struggle & scream. Even then it never occurred

[124v]

to me that anything was wrong. In fact I said within myself how easily I could have swallowed the stuff & made no fuss about it.

Then all was still—the two sat down at desk. Clink of money. The proceedings all through appeared to me queer but my anxiety for my own safety prevented me attaching that importance that under other circumstances I should. Want of sleep & continual murmuring seemed to have dulled my comprehension.

Peeping through keyhole not a very pleasant occupation especially when just touching the skulls of some poor creatures who probably committed self destruction. Were the owners of the skulls come to keep me company. Noise behind. One skull displaced. O how dreadfully tired & faint I felt—the place smelt as if I actually were in midst of the dead.

The two worthies softly approached sofa—the Doctor pronounced life to be extinct. Disease of the heart exclaimed the precious rascal. Of course answered the amiable husband. I instinctively recoiled & fell knocking over skulls & bottles. Womanlike I screamed. Not with fright but for simple reason that I happened to alight on something sharp.

My greatest enemy would have had pity.

Key missed—Doctor asked in rather a shaking voice who was there. Doctor went to find a tool to open door. Husband went into garden.

With a glance at the poor dead woman I fled up to my own room & locked the door.

The Doctor he was not a D^r really—only called so from courtesy—proper form of address was M^r—Surgeon with initials M.R.C.S. saw it in Medical Directory.

Lady found dead some hours after by housekeeper on her return. Whether she was a party to the plot or not I could never acertain. [sic]

Hurried funeral—no one attended but the 2 poisoners.

[123v]

Dr. T. made no inquiries about the laudanum. I concluded he was reserving his wrath—the suspense. He found a more cautious way of letting me know he knew it was I.

My husband & he great friends. Easy to have me sent to an Asylum. More than sufficient evidence against me I will candidly admit. I made up my mind to say nothing to my husband & wait issue of events.

Felt as if I had assisted to murder the poor woman. If I had taken that little bottle I should in all probability have taken an overdose. The destiny that ruled over me then has not made my end very shapely. If God would only give us a glimpse of the troubles & sorrows during time he contemplates fashioning us & give us option of refusing how eagerly would I refuse to become a human being. But I was like rest of mankind not consulted.

Before I resume the surgery affair I will still further digress & touch as lightly as possible on my first & greatest bereavement.

'Tis many years since my first husband Capt. W. Mackeith Master Mariner & owner was drowned. I was then 17.

Lying awake that night heard my name pronounced in my husband's voice in one long expiring sigh—not even prefaced by any endearing expression. Wind began to rise. Before midnight it was blowing a gale and a half. Next night 3 mins to 8 leaning on chair—overshadowed by dark & a misty cloud—figure of husband occupied chair—said 'My Darling Wife, do not grieve for me for you shall never see me again in this world.'

My tongue, right arm & right side paralised & quite dead.

Next day news of his death. Shock so great that for close on 2 years I dragged on a miserable existence in a Lunatic Asylum.

[122v]

Could tell many incidents but fear putting your credulity to the test.

Now I will resume the surgery adventure. It clings to me like a nightmare.

Mr. T. after funeral came up & said he had a serious charge against Mrs M a person of very dangerous tendencies strange & peculiar ideas & habits not fit to be at large—bland tone of voice—so refined <?> he seemed the most reverent and kind individual in existence. All this assumed to acertain [*sic*] how much I heard & knew.

I did not keep him long in suspense as to what I thought of him—told him he & his friend had murdered the Lady & if he attempted to induce my husband to consent to his proposal I should relate all I knew to the proper authorities—said he stood a better chance of being locked up & strictly watched than I did.

My Husband said it only showed how mad I was to conceive such a thing & that the woman died of heart disease on return from consulting a doctor. I said I had seen them pour the mixture down her throat—if the stomach was analised my 'conception' as he was pleased to call it would be called by some other name.

Dr —— turned pale—consulted my husband alone. All my husband said when he returned was that I must keep very quiet & not excite myself. Doctor would forget my tampering & send me a soothing draught, which I promptly refused. That awful house—those gloomy rooms.

The conclusion—invitations from Mr. M.'s friends. My dislike to mixing in society. I lived alone or almost alone. Horror of crowds. Would never walk in streets if I could help it.

You will naturally say my mind was in an unhealthy state & that accounted for my hearing voices—but that had nothing to do with it. Regret that I did not cry out & save the woman's life. Got worse instead of better. At last I could not lay down either night or day. When I attempted to feeling of someone standing or bending over me.

[121v]

My husband sometimes remained at home to complete some musical composition—constantly obliged to suppress my agitation. I drew armchair to window so closely that even a shadow would have no chance of standing room. Sleeping draught but light uneasy slumber.

At this time my husband was offered an appointment as bandmaster in Sussex—he did duties of clerk during day and in evening instructed his men in music. 2 evenings he devoted to private pupils. I remained in London 2 weeks after he left.

One evening at 8.30 waiting for postman[4]—suddenly heard fluttering as of a bird in a cage just behind me—thick greyish vapour descending from ceiling. In bedroom—communicating with sitting-room by folding doors. Very large lofty & gloomy—vapour there too—strange whispers from 4 corners of room. I was perfectly calm & collected & not at all afraid.

Presently a voice—of a woman raised to the ordinary pitch—yet voice from a distance & as if coming through a <word?> & speaker looking at me all the time. Tone of suppressed anger. 'You—wicked—woman.'

I fled. As I went past the bedroom door I saw sitting on the bed the face in profile of the long haired lady—with alteration that her hair was now bound up—the dress was the same.

In the street—terror of feeling her hand on my shoulder. No hat or mantle. My one great desire to preserve a calm manner & appearance. I had walked or I may say run a considerable distance from home & in direction of Regent's Park before I became aware of my half dressed condition.

To return impossible—so I decided to remain in shadow as much as possible till my nerves got settled—No money or I would have taken a bed for the night.

Very late—I knew I was an object of suspicion to the policeman on beat.

[120v]

Knowing how utterly impossible it would be to remain out all night I retraced my steps.

Found no light—prayed God for strength—& feeling more calm went in & lighted lamp.

In bedroom vapour & lady gone. Still one more strange & unaccountable thing—my right hand was or appeared to be covered with blood. I washed it in several waters but no change—whole hand deep crimson extending to first joint of the wrist—my left hand usual colour but appeared much whiter when contrasted with the other.

My first thought was that perhaps I was going to have a fever—but strange that symptoms should begin in the hand—never recollected a case of the kind.

Naturally alarmed & tried to account for it. Not indigestion. Nothing or very little to digest. Often fasted for days & would now if I were not questioned about it & compelled to eat.

We eat too much. Less meat more brains. Not a bad principal [*sic*] especially in an Establishment like this where there is such a want of the latter commodity.

Suddenly it flashed upon me—painful circumstance many years before—now horribly vivid—I will give you the facts though I know they will not reflect any credit upon me.

After I left the Asylum I decided to go to the Seaside for change of scene & air. (I was a private patient—the money came out of my own pocket. My husband left me very well provided for.)

I engaged a woman to attend to me. Whether she told anything I can't say—but people looked strangely at me as I passed. I walked on remote part of beach but not a little surprised to see heads of men & women every now & again popping up from behind rocks & sandhills all evidently watching my movements. Very unpleasant but I could not interfere the place was open to everyone. There only one week—persuaded myself to make the best of everything when it occurred to me that I had brought a 6-chambered revolver that had been given to Capt. MacKeith.

[119v]

Why could not I shoot some of those 'seagulls' the white plumage would look so pretty in Hats. I unpacked the box & was examining the chambers when in rushed a woman of about my own height—& tried to snatch the revolver. In a moment I had divined her thoughts. She thought I was about to do something rash. I asked her to leave the room. She refused unless I gave up the 'pistol' as she called it. The insolent interference was quite enough. I would put her out. Little she knew with whom she had to deal. In a moment I had her by the throat. She was but a baby in my hands. First having half strangled her I threw her down some steps on the passage, down which she rolled & lay there. I regret to say I did not attempt to pick her up again. She never recovered consciousness & died soon after. She had been asked by my servant to 'keep an eye on me' while she was away. There was of course great commotion—an enquiry—an account of which I am not going to worry you with. My holiday at an end & for some months very little peace in my household.

This is the only way in which I can account for the stain.

The stain gradually disappeared. Not so the vapour—which

appeared again about 1 hour after ascending from floor in little spiral columns & assuming that appearance on ceiling that frost does on window glass. No voices but dropping of water till late in the morning.

I turned my back on that doomed house. 'Mistaken Souls that dream of Heaven'⁵ the troubled mind accused me.

One more incident before I took my departure. I had lost a long black silk glove—searched everywhere—in vain. One night I had gone out to get something for my husband's supper. I stood beside the railings of a garden square <word?> wondering why some people imagine that the moon is inhabited when I perceived a small dark object floating over my head gradually growing larger & larger untill [sic] it appeared about half as large as the Court attached to Bethnall [sic] House & as black as ink—darkness against bright sky—felt touch on shoulder—put my hand up & found my glove.

That is another mystery that will never be solved at least by me.

[118v]

I leave you awhile to ponder over what I have written while I take myself to

Sussex

Not the place I should have selected. My Husband liked the place & people. I seldom had his society. For a considerable time I did not miss him—furnishing & arranging domestic matters. Took a month before we were quite settled.

During that time I was better. Voices & apparitions gone I hoped never to return. I slept well & altogether a great improvement. House new, furnature [sic] new—excitement new.

One evening I went out on an exploring expedition, after walking about 5 miles sat down to rest. Suddenly I became possessed with a strong desire to be home again—felt as if something dreadful had occurred or was about to occur. I jumped up. As I did so I heard the dear sweet voice of my little daughter say 'Mother Mother.' I had been thinking of her & wondering how she looked. She promised to grow up very pretty. She was with her sister at school by family arrangement. Vacations spent with their father's mother.

Home late having missed way—preoccupied & sad. A letter awaiting me containing the sad tidings of death of my favourite child. She died of scarlatina fever.[6]

Job's wife's mood angelic compared with mine because I really did curse God without any prompting.[7]

I shed no tears. After all only a short time must elapse before I see her. I have a perfect understanding with God & believe that the method I shall adopt to produce that everlasting sleep will not be disapproved of by him.

I sat alone in my Husband's study—darkness of despair—dry sorrow—eyeballs hot as fire—no sound but ticking of clock.

Suddenly a shriek of mocking laughter. At first thought it was some of the <word?> with

[118r]

that curiosity for which they are famous. With my usual desire to acertain [sic] a cause I went into all the rooms.

Return to the Study—a bright fire & a still brighter lamplight. Tried to read. A large pierglass on mantelpiece opposite. On table a violin in case, close to table a music stand with instruction book. Brass musical instruments in corners—on walls my guitar.

Room well & very comfortably furnished—table covered with rich crimson cloth—window hangings of same. 2 easy chairs handsome carpet & hearthrug. Everything to please the eye & sense. Nothing to depress or cause one to feel gloomy.

Presently loud note or sound from the trombone after string of violin sent forth a rather loud sound—more like the snapping of a string than anything else—leaves of music book distinctly turned.

Great Heavens what could it be? My eyes fell on pierglass—reflection of female form gliding towards door—guitar touched but faintly.

Stealthy tread outside in passage as if hesitating & whispering in consultation whether to enter. Haunted or mad! And after the dreadful time that I had in London & the way in which I managed to control myself together with the tact & energy that I displayed in removing from London I could come to no other conclusion than that I was haunted by either devils or angels.

How could I have been mad. It was I who selected every article of furnature [*sic*] & superintended the arrangements. I was obliged to meet with people in a business way & converse with them in a businesslike manner. Yet no one noticed anything peculiar about me. I should have observed it if they had. I was and am a mystery to myself.

I think there are few women on earth possessed of such power of control over self

[117v]

or concealment of feelings as I am.

Now the domestic machinery was revolving smoothly these dreadful fiends were come to torment & goad me to madness.

But to resume … I did not wait long for my ghostly visitants to enter. I left the room & proceeded to light up the whole house— even to the back kitchen. 4 rooms upstairs and 3 down. I sat on top landing & had a view of all the doors.

After a little I heard faint & low the voice of my dear dead daughter call apparently from the breakfast-parlour at back of study & on the ground floor. 'Mother darling, come away with me now.' I rushed downstairs. Voice seemed outside window— she still kept calling me from garden. I ran into garden. All still & calm. Air soft & warm.

Inhabitants chiefly seafaring—their families in bed before 9 & at any time when on land you could hear the plash plash of the tide.

My husband was never very demonstrative in his affections— so taken up by his new friends—more & more careless of my society. The fact is I think he was half afraid of me. Another thing he was full of anecdotes and 'good company.' Out of 12 months he never spent 4 nights at home with me. Never home before midnight. We were seldom together except at meal times. Separate bedrooms by mutual arrangement. My servant went home to sleep after 6 o'clock. Her husband was a sailor.

On my return from garden I found my husband had returned. He wanted to know what I meant by having lights all over the house. I told him exactly what had occurred. He said I must have dreamed it. Examined violin & other instruments. Found nothing the matter with them. Said I ought to have someone to stay with me during his absence.

[117r]

Soon found I had greater difficulties to contend with. Rest broken so often during night to remain in bed impossible. No alternative but to wander all over the house or sit at drawing-room window & gladly rest my head on the cold stone.

What a wretched miserable woman I felt—go where I would there were the voices of people long since dead & of those I knew were alive constantly talking to me—sometimes imploringly sometimes menacingly—crowding together or scattered all over the house—crouching in corners. Words seemed to issue from the ground.

My child's voice I particularly noticed was more clear more distinct than the others. She always appeared to be alone—always same words requesting me to accompany her.

This continued for several weeks—except that for some hours every day I heard nothing whatever & what peace I had.

Very very thin—appetite altered for worse—felt quite worn out. No one to observe change but my husband & I would not see a doctor. No bodily ailment & I would not think of telling him how wretchedly my days & nights were spent.

One night I sat in breakfast-room when I heard the feeble cry of an infant just over my head—close to my ear—or right away at top of house.

When that ceaced [sic], a strangely peculiar singing noise as if someone were humming some horrid ditty—breaking off & beginning again.

If I rushed into garden, wind whistled the unfinished portion in my ear, untill [sic] I could liken my head to an old ruin through which the wind rushed at will.

Heard a full band play some delightful music from 2 to 4 in early morning. I could even remember a portion of a tune for an hour together.

[116v]

One particular night I was quite free from any sound—returned to bed about eleven if not to sleep to rest.

Must describe how I was positioned.

I lay with my feet towards window—close to window a wardrobe with plate glass door—& in which I could see any passing object—drew a pedestal cupboard to bedside as was my usual habit & on it placed my reading lamp.

Had read about 15 minutes when sudden rush at window— before I could jump up those dreadful voices commenced again. Counted 7 distinct voices—from feeble cry of a young infant to the deep tones of a man's voice. Scramble to get nearest the glass. Loud awful voices. Could not distinguish words very clearly at first. Confused babble—persistent determination.

Cry of baby most heartrending as if in dreadful agony.

Voices of women (of our own family) accused me of having committed every offence that comes within the meaning of the 'Ten Commandments.'

For the first time I answered back—denying—when the awful deep voice of the man spoke in such an accusing manner— 'Hidden Children—Hidden Children'—raising voice at 'hidden' and lowering it at 'Children' like the rumbling of distant thunder and ending with a groan. Words echoed behind my head so I was attacked at both ends of room.

After a little time I felt [*sic*] getting stronger & I said I would not allow even the devil & all his imps to get the better of me—I would not be conquered but would open the window. I sat up in my bed—preparatory to getting out—when I saw in wardrobe door my dear little daughter. She looked pale & rather thin—her eyes very brilliant—she wore the ordinary house dress of a child of 8. I got only a glance of her reflection as she crossed—the other voices almost inaudible at this time.

[116r]

Got out of bed & raised window. Only moon and stars to see. Rush of pure air revived me. Swash of tide against rocks grateful & pleasant sensation.

I can't say how long I sat at open window—scene so beauti- ful—on sea vessels of various tonage [*sic*] passing—reminding me of passing away of souls.

To left high white bare cliffs almost perpendicular—sandy beach in light of moon like a broad white ribbon—favourite walk of mine in my quiet moments—lights from different steam- boats—red harbour lights made a pretty picture.

At last I shut out peace & prepared to encounter my late tormentors should they again trouble me. How easily, you will say, I could put off all traces of my recent disturbance & how indifferent I appear in anticipation of my second attack.

You will perhaps think I ought to have occupied same room as my husband or gone to him when voices so annoying—I should like to have done so sometimes—but he locked his bedroom door—we had separate sleeping rooms.

It was my own suggestion I admit but I think his acceptance of arrangement was too hasty. He took my words in a literal sense—whether he was glad or otherwise I could not learn. I only know that he performed his allotted part to perfection. He said 'go to my own room & not bother him.'

I had the advantage that I could wander <?> all over the house & while away the time as I liked. Always pleased when morning dawned.

I went out on 3 or 4 occasions to spend the day or evening with wife of my husband's greatest & most intimate friend.

But the effort to preserve a calm exterior & collected manner before strangers whom I met on these occassions (sic) too much for me.

[115v]

Dreadful tune dinning in my ears all the time.

At last I refused to go out altogether. Husband annoyed. Said it would be unpleasant for him as he must give some reason for my refusal. I would not let the people know my life was so haunted. I still attributed my annoyance to being haunted.

How could I possibly be insane. No woman on earth could be more cautious more circumspect than I. How could I always control my feelings before people—tradespeople for instance—who called for orders. Messengers from my husband's office—all these I was obliged to see myself & send back correct answers.

Another night to spend in wretchedness—Determined headstrong defiant as I proved myself to be I must succumb at last. I could not eat, sleep, rest, mentally or bodily by night or day.

I knew I was really getting worse & that I could not always keep myself in subjection. Often a strong desire to take to smashing things just to relieve my feelings—especially under the bitterness of my husband's indifference. I blame him very much for my trouble.

And although it is wrong & in bad taste to speak ill of the dead I cannot help alluding now & again to the cowardly manner in which I have been treated by him.

I always kept a light burning all night in the hall all night [*sic*] & always of course in my bedroom. I was reading there before my husband came home—ears stuffed with cotton wool—strip of flannel under my chin.

Undisturbed till long after my husband came home. Hoped it would continue—but not to be. Something new was planned: some new and startling mode of torture deliberated on.

Slight noise as if fly had dropped on open page—not a fly but a tiny white specklike atom of snowflake. Remained on book a moment—then out of its centre issued a tiny

[115r]

column of sulphurous smoke—faintest possible sound which cotton wool did not prevent me from hearing.

This happened several times. I was most disagreeably impressed—tried to account for it—as I always do for any unusual voice or appearance. At first thought it was a soul passing away & if so the journey could not have been a pleasant one.

Again that it was a presentiment of what was to come & perhaps the latter conclusion was most correct. Why sulphur should aid in its disappearance I dare not express an opinion.

After that voices again at window.

Overhead a regular party discussing my merits and demerits—my mother-in-law—my sister-in-law—my daughter who is now alive—& my brother-in-law, with other voices that I did not recognise. They discussed me fearfully with exception of my daughter & her uncle who took my part in a most decided manner. I heard every word they said distinctly. Seemed to be at a round table. As their voices grew louder & angrier those at window more indistinct.

To my right were two strangers standing at a square opening in the wall. Man & woman. Like the ticket office at railway station.

Woman plainly dressed in black like bible-women who visit amongst poor. Man also in black with white band round his neck.

Woman tried to make me believe that I should go to her Church in seductive tones. I answered rather roughly. She said I could only go to Heaven by joining Church of Rome & through Intercession of Virgin. I scolded her—she took it all in good part—kept turning to the man for his opinion & then again address [*sic*] me in most persuasive manner. At last I threw the book at her—asking why the man

[114v]

didn't join in the interesting (?) conversation. She said he was a Jesuit & seldom spoke, was much interested in me. I was so very good, so very pretty. I jumped out of bed. The man looked & smiled, said they would give me their address in London. I wrote it on the wallpaper. 54 or 57 Russell Square. When I ceaced [*sic*] writing they had disappeared.

The man at window cried 'Hidden Children' again. I rushed out & ran to my husband's door—locked—called, no answer. At last I lost all control over myself & screamed to be let in—still no answer. What O what would become of me. Expected that dreadful man to come behind perhaps grasp me.

Never since the world began up to present time did mortal woman ever suffer the awful frienzy [*sic*] of a maddened brain. No madhouse ever yet errected [*sic*] or peopled etc. Every drop of blood in my Body felt like fire—temples felt as if throbbing would rend my head in two.

I ran down & got the meat chopper & smashed in panels of door—put in my hand & turned the key. I was inside. What a picture met my view. Husband trembling at raised window—never moved nor uttered sound.

My first impulse was to kill him there & then. I raised weapon with that intention—scream of 'Mother come away' arrested my hand. My child's voice saved me from becoming a 'murderer.' The scene—splinters of wood—open window. Many a time it glides before me. I threw chopper through window & ran out of room into garden & reached riverside—nothing on but night-gown & thick felt dressing gown. Cold morning air calmed me. I returned—found Husband in study writing—his first words were 'You will be the death of me'

[114r]

& I firmly believe he spoke the truth. But then he brought it all on himself. I will not enter into details regarding my husband's illness & its unhappy result. I am now keenly alive to that disgraceful outburst of mad passion.

When I look around on the majority of patients in this house & see the care the attention lavished upon them consequent on the display of some petty vulgar temper that they wilfully & viciously give way to & don't make effort to control but feed & encourage it with no other object in their mean composition than attract notice of 'Matron' & 'Doctor' & receive special notice & special words of mild reproof which only encourages them the more in their wickedness....

But then I will not try to contrast myself with such people—it would be too utterly absurd—position and circumstances of most of patients differ much from what mine has been.

The suppression of passion a difficult thing—fighting the devil—a dreadful battle. Many a victory have I gained & unfortunately I have been defeated but not often.

Husband went to his business after noon. Doctor and Matron called. I was perfectly collected—knew his intention—to send me to Asylum—but Doctor could detect no traces of insanity. I decided to go to London & see a Doctor myself.

Voices again. 'It is one o'clock & your husband is dead.'

Husband stayed at hotel—never came near me.

At night I sat in study—a cheerful room—more colour about it—strains of music—as if musical box on window ledge—played 'Blue Bells of Scotland'[8] till 6 a.m. I thought it was held by someone passing. I rather liked it.

Voice of my little daughter again—also of my sister. Heart-rending crying. How I wish

[113v]

I were possessed of better descriptive powers—how much more readable this story would be! My sister's voice told me our mother was dead—first time I had heard of it. She said she died in April & was buried between George Henry <?> & herself. She had met none of our relatives was quite alone & such a long dark way to go. I asked her if she was in Heaven. No answer but her grief dreadful something appaling. [sic] Should I go to Heaven when I died. She said never never never. Well, I thought that is certainly not a very bright prospect for me to contemplate. Music playing all this time. I wrote that day to know if Mother alive. Received answer that she had died 9 months previously & buried where my sister had told me. That hymn called 'We shall meet to part no more'[9] a delusion & not to be relied on because my sister was quite long enough to have discovered her relations.

It was now 9 p.m.—I had some Tea & Toast—everything so nicely prepared. I certainly had a lovely home but 'fleeting are the joys of earth.'[10] Night fine. I went for short walk. Voice saying 'Violet, you are a fool!' thought it was my husband. No one there. I turned & ran. At my door—voice didn't accompany me in—but ran down road to entrance gate of the Cross Swords <?> & appeared to stand in middle of road & scream.

In my room. Every object that my eye rested upon spoke of some awful change—every article of furniture appeared to wear a mournful look. I sat down to read an amusing book—I have a copy of it given me by one of the nurses—title is Mr & Mrs Spoopendyke[11]—American. Some very amusing short tales in it. Nice fire burning. Number of pictures in room. Figures in picture moving as if alive. At first thought it might be the position of the lamp. I will describe it—if you have never heard of anything of the kind before it will enable you to judge if insanity had anything to do with it.

(1) Neapolitan lady under luxuriant foliage—guitar in hand. I saw her bony

[113r]

long white fingers moving over the strings. Eyes move—head raised when necessary to take high note—no sound—breeze now and then stirred lace on dress & elbows—leaves rustling.

(2) Scene on Coast of France. 'The Expected Return'—groups of fisherwomen round ancient cross. Woman rocking in grief at foot of cross—child trying to draw her apron away—another wringing her hands—mouth opening at times. Woman with long telescope—pushing it in or pulling it out. 'Her capstrings appeared to have a little amusement on their own account.' One man kneeling & praying.

(3) A Winter Song—Robin—throat throbbing bill opening.

(4) The 3 Generations—Xmas Day assembly in drawing <?> room.

(5) Little girl washing a dog in tub, '& judging from expression of his face, he would not become a candidate for enforcement of sanitary laws amongst dogs.'

I took the lamp & went to each one in turn—felt quite pleased at this discovery—something to amuse me at all events. The thought struck me that daylight would bring them back to their original habits, i.e. remaining perfectly still—but daylight made no difference—for weeks for months they kept me amused—nor could I understand why others could not see as I did.

On evening of 3rd day husband, his friend Mr S. & the Doctor came to see me. I felt very much inclined to indulge my feelings of suppressed rage against my husband for having shamefully left me & against his friend for having aided and abetted him in his wickedness. Yet with my usual command over self I kept my temper—not any of the three could detect anything amiss. I knew if I once gave way to temper it would immediately be put down to madness. After that my doom was sealed. The Doctor touched on the broken door but I drew his attention to the picture of the little girl washing the dog. He did not appear to understand me & the subject dropped.

After they had gone dreadful depression as if my husband lay dead in one of the upper

[109v]

rooms & I actually could not rest until I went to see although I knew he was not in the house. During 12 months I did not get 20 nights' sleep. I daresay Dr Will or Dr Miller can not be made to believe this & possibly will not credit many things written here. That is their loss not mine.

Gave up reading to study my pictures—sometimes quite free from gloomy thoughts—at others in depth of depression. My daughter's voice seemed not to expect me to respond—as if she were getting tired of my constant non-compliance. Idea of getting poison. Only one chemist's—but no matter what I asked for they said they had not any just then. No desire to disfigure myself in case daughter should not recognise me—therefore I should take poison or shoot myself through heart.

Miserable night chased by voices & singing. Husband much opposed to my going to London alone. I did not say goodbye to him—felt too indignant.

Not many minutes in train when I wished myself back again. Mid-day express from Lewes after 9 a.m. from Brighton—dark tunnels—one very long one before Croydon.

Travelled 2ⁿᵈ class & alone in compartment. Speed of train increased till I expected every moment it would come off the rails. Those devilish voices again commenced to torment me— quite close to my ear. Wild unearthly shrieks of that awful engine pierced through brain like a sharp instrument. I thought I was dead & that great monster dragging me with others down to an unknown world perhaps to Hell.

I beat the sides of the carriage—surrounded on every side by voices—tried to beat them away. Horrid low mocking laughter— suffocating—faint—dying. I was mangled in imagination.

[109r]

I could not last much longer. Who is that standing in the compartment? Yes there was a man with his back to the carriage window. He was dressed like a porter—viz. cord trousers & jacket—the usual cap & in his hand he held a lighted lantern—glare lighted the carriage previously in darkness. His face the 3 lengths of an ordinary man's face, colour a dirty leaden or deathly colour that you see in faces of people who are dead about one week.

His eyes fixed on me with such a diabolical scowl—as he commenced to back out at the door I heard myself scream. I was found lying in carriage on my face & quite insensible. Carried into waiting room or refreshment room I forget which at Croydon & treated with great kindness. I wore a black chip hat¹² & it was much crushed by the fall but otherwise without a scratch. I firmly believe that man was the devil.

A lady took charge of me. Before I fainted I must have snatched at my 'guitar' that I brought with me in order to have the strings seen to.

At London Bridge the Lady sent for a cab. I told the driver to go to the nearest 'Coffee House.' I got some tea, rested for about an hour & set out to look for lodgings.

A Policeman sent me to the house of a mate of his whose

wife was a dressmaker. Very nice people & kind to me. Made efforts to go & see a doctor but turned giddy & frightened the moment I passed the threshold. Noise too much for me. To this day noise of a railway whistle & rush of an engine frightens me very much.

Stayed there one week—never slept—men's & women's voices kept annoying me—as when at home.

In the daytime as bad—to hide my feelings I kept in my room. I thought the people of the house did not observe anything strange in my manner but they must have.

[108v]

'Shall we leave the light burning? Oh yes it will be all right.' It was my own light. Well I managed to get out one day & I did find a doctor. I described my state to him. He looked very serious, said my best plan would be to return home at once—that I had a very disordered mind & was *dancing* on pretty feet to a madhouse. I should try & agree with my husband, go out every day, live generously & mix with my fellow creatures.

I returned home—but this time I got into a carriage where there were a number of other people. I will here bring my troubles to a close. If it has no other effect it will at least let you see what a woman with a determined will is capable of enduring.

As to my future that is wrapped in mystery. My present prospects are not very bright but perhaps the dawn is not far off.

Trusting that you will make every allowance for the many mistakes & scratchings that you will have met with

    I shall sign
   Myself
     'Satisfied'

     'A Vision'

I asked God once to give me a glimpse of Heaven Hell & the Middle State—if there was a Middle State & this is what I saw.

I found myself on a very broad road on high elevation from which I could see a black & barren country—thousands of miles—not one green leaf—every tree & shrub blackened &

bare. To my right a dark sullen looking river—possibly the Styx
& to the left

[108r]

a dark & impenetrable wood. Peering from between the trees
white anxious & emaciated faces all evidently trying to get away
from each other.

Outside forest—a muddy greyish mist over river & whole
country like the murky dawn of a winter's morning.

At the bottom I looked up & saw coming down old & young
women & men coming down to join the thousands of workers.

This was Hell. No fire & brimstone—only punishment carrying heavy loads of earth from one place to another. Ground burning hot—pierced with holes through which I could see the fire
burning or 'hell's fire.'

The Devil had discretion enough to conceal it from his victims'
eyes—the intense heat underfoot caused them to be constantly
running about.

His Satanic Majesty nowhere to be seen.

I entered the dark forest—before & behind I could see thousands of every age sex & class hastening away from hell preparatory to entering the Middle State.

Still dark—some fell & could not get up—no [sic] one person
appeared to wait to assist another—but went on headlong, pushing & scrambling & groaping [sic] their way. Dressed in black,
loose gowns with a cord round the waist.

Light in distance. At last we were quite out of the darkness.
Patches of cultivated land—trees & shrubs—young leaves bud-
ding. People remained here, sowing seeds & planting young
trees—rolling large stones—making nets. As quickly as work
completed they undid it again. All working as if their salvation
was at stake—as of course it was.

I left this place—path wider—country better & richer—long
dark place to pass through not

[107v]

unlike the Tunnel I have spoken of.

Different set of people. Cheerful yet anxious. 'I shall feel
happy when I get there & not till then.' Dressed in scarlet with
girdle. Lamp in hand like that carried by the 'Ten Virgins.'

Presently a world of dazzling brightness—we had arrived in Heaven—Joy, gladness. First words I heard were 'For Ever with the King.' Whole multitudes began to sing. They at same time began to ascend steps of white marbel [*sic*] to immense hall studded with precious stones. As they entered each hung up his or her lamp on hooks of gold & went into another & longer & richer place where myriads of angels unrobed them—put on a white one threaded with gold. But my dress was not touched—I was not even noticed.

Leaving that hall of beauty I found myself alone.

Hundreds of castles of dazzling brightness apparently composed of gems & precious stones. Lovely flowers & birds—trees & fruit—marble roads covered with crimson & gold cloth interwoven. Grand procession forming. First carriage drawn by 20 horses abreast & 20 deep—horses covered with crimson & gold. Coachman <word?> a mass of gold bands—fringe with scarlet white & gold. Carriage picked out blue & gold covered with crimson cloth. No footman. All other equipages like it except one & that was the one in which God sat. Behind each carriage a regiment representing every nation of this world.

Heaven appeared to be several worlds rolled into one—for of course I could see for millions of miles around.

Last grand carriage was a sight. Shaped like a wind <?> barge with a large square piece <?> cut out of centre. Massive carved pillar at bow & stern & at each side & they supported white velvet hangings trimmed with very deep & heavy gold fringe.

[107r]

Drawn by 160 horses—half covered with white & gold, half with crimson & gold. No coachman. The place where God ought to be was covered over with most magnificent violet velvet cloth with gold fringe. I thought within myself 'Well, even in heaven things are not quite perfect.' I was disappointed & deeply troubled. But then the Bible says 'No man hath seen God at any time'[13] & I was of course a mortal.

I will just remark that all this belief about meeting friends & dead relatives in Heaven is I think doubtful, as I never saw in either hell, middle state or Heaven anyone I knew on earth.

And indeed when you come to think there are a great number

of people here who would not feel at all rejoiced at meeting some of their earthly acquaintances. Even in Heaven. I think they are better apart. At the same time I expect to meet my child when I enter the other world—when we shall go hand in hand to the golden city.

Trusting to a future happy state I shall endeavour to make the best of this,

V. M.

(*Extracted fr. original doct Sundays 2nd & 9th Decr 1888.*)

NOTES

1 "M.R.C.S." denotes member of the Royal College of Surgeons. The home this surgeon owns might be a Georgian building, with an upstairs drawing-room.

2 The British Temperance Movement was vigorous throughout Anstey's lifetime, although as he was writing *The Statement of Stella Maberly* it suffered a temporary setback with the defeat of the Liberal Party in the 1895 election.

3 Punishable abortions were those that could not be justified as last-ditch interventions to save the mother's life, and maybe the baby's life too.

4 At this time in London the last postal delivery of the day might be made between 7.45 and 8.45pm.

5 This is the opening line of a hymn by Isaac Watts (1674-1748) which emphasises the futility of those who do not lead Christian lives professing Christian belief.

6 For as long as most Victorians could remember, scarlet fever had been one of the most feared diseases in the land; the worst epidemics were between 1840 and 1880.

7 While Job was exercising great patience in the face of terrible trials inflicted upon himself and his family, his wife urged him to "curse God, and die" (Job 2:9).

8 This is a Scottish folk song which Anstey is likely to have known from a very young age. His father's family was Scottish and his mother was a piano teacher.

9 The line is from a consolatory rhyme of unknown authorship, "On that bright immortal shore / We shall meet to part no more," which

is often found on gravestones. (It is, however, the "bright immortal shore" which is likelier to have featured in the hymn remembered here.)

10   This line appears in Elizabeth O. Dannelly's Cactus; or, Thorns and Blossoms (New York: Atlantic Publishing, 1873), p. 353.

11   A collection of Stanley Huntley's extremely popular sketches, The Spoopendyke Papers, was published in New York in 1883. They are comedies of marital misunderstanding, in which Mrs Spoopendyke tries but fails to please her impatient and irascible husband.

12   This is an example of the fashionable headwear of the time, probably trimmed with feathers and flowers.

13   A line from the Gospels (John 1:18)

APPENDIX II: Violet Millar's Statement

Violet Millar's Statement

As far as my memory will allow—that I then & now believe

'Unravel' what will at best be a 'tangled skein.'

Notwithstanding some things will appear so impossible, remember everything happened just as I have written it.

Only merit in this narrative is truth.

Presentiment—Sleeplessness.

The selfpity—appreciation of horror of situation.

The sham logic—attempt to explain delusions by natural causes

stock quotations (but here <?> a half educated woman)

Selfpraise—'I am not a —'

dread of dwelling on a scene

the half consciousness of insanity—candid admissions that appearances warranted it.

Wish that God would give us option of refusing life beforehand.

The sense of digressing.

Attempts to reason with herself

But I know that all this was assumed.

Dislike to society & pity for her loneliness

horror of crowds

[49v]

You will naturally say my mind in an unhealthy state & that perhaps accounted for it—but that had nothing to do with it.

Belief in being watched.

In a moment I divined her thought

hint at suicide

Was I haunted or mad. How could. I have been mad.

Pride in her own selfcontrol

I was & am a mystery to myself

insistence on detail

You will perhaps think

Effort to preserve a calm exterior

desire to smash things for relief.

Keenly alive to that disgraceful outburst of mad passion.

Wish for more descriptive powers that story might be more readable—

The delirium of the animated pictures—

APPENDIX III: AN EVIL SPIRIT

In the British Library Anstey archive, Additional MS 54308 contains five film scenarios, all apparently prepared between March 1915 and March 1916. The third of the five, "An Evil Spirit," was written over the space of ten days in the middle of February 1916. The text of this (occupying fos 110-143) is transcribed below, together with the front matter (fos 107-09). The numerals in brackets, from [107] onwards, refer to the numbered folio sheets of the manuscript; the numerals in parentheses, from (1) onwards, are the numbers of the scenes.

[107]

Scenario for Film

An Evil Spirit
by
F. Anstey
(founded on his story 'The Statement of Stella Maberly')
In   Parts[1]

[108]

List & Description of Principal Characters

1. *Stella Maberly*
Age, in the opening scene at Asylum, about 30. Appearance, still beautiful, but with streaks of premature grey in her black hair.
Age at beginning of story, 18. Afterwards about 22. A tall slender brunette, rather stormy & passionate-looking.
{n.b. I do not imagine that Miss Lillah McCarthy[2] could be engaged for this part, but I mention her as the ideal type for it.}

2. *Evelyn Heseltine*
Age, at beginning of story 18—afterwards about 22.

Tall, not necessarily as tall as Stella, but not much shorter. A complete contrast to her in other ways. Fairhaired with an expression of sweetness & innocence.

After the transformation this expression shows a subtle change at times but only when she is alone with Stella or unobserved.

{Type would be Miss Nina Severing, or Miss Lydia Bilbrooke.[3]}

3. *The Evil Spirit*
A shadowy form in black gauzy drapery, with a handsome but voluptuous & slightly cruel face.

4. *Mrs Maitland*
Age about 55. A ~~comfort~~ pleasant placid well-bred looking woman.

5. *Hugh Dallas*
Age about 26. Tall, dark, goodlooking. Cleanshaven. A man who is fond of sport & country life generally, but has wider interests & tastes.

~~6. Stella's Father~~
~~Age about 50. A typical Country Squire. Handsome, with dark hair beginning to turn grey.~~

6. *Stella's Stepmother*
Age about 40. Goodlooking & not unkindly, though her manner to Stella shows that there is no real affection or sympathy between them.

[109]
7. *The Medical Superintendent*
Middle-aged, grave & kindly.

8. *The Rector*
Age about 60. Portly, & dignified, with an expression generally benignant but capable of great sternness.

9. *A Coachman*
Elderly, fond of his horses & the dog, devoted to Evelyn.

10. *A Chauffeur*

11. *A Station-master*

12. *A Porter*

13. Small child at girls' school.

14. M^rs. Chichester, the Schoolmistress. Age 55. Greyhaired, stately-looking, but sympathetic.

also

Butler, maids & other servants when the situation requires them.

Guests at Country Garden Party, & Wedding.

People in Congregation at Village Church.

School-girls.

[110]

Leader[4]
Stella Maberly has been found guilty of murder, but reprieved on the ground of insanity. After some years' confinement as a criminal lunatic, feeling herself about to die, she tells the Medical Superintendent how & why she became a murderess.

Fade into

(1)

Scene A bedroom in a Criminal Lunatic Asylum.
Action Stella, still young & with traces of great beauty, though her hair ~~is patched~~ shows streaks of grey here & there, is sitting up in bed, supported by pillows, speaking earnestly but without any excitement in her manner to the Medical Superintendent. At the opening he is listening sympathetically, but rather to humour her than because he expects a story of any coherence or interest. {But at each stage of the story when this scene recurs, his manner is that of a man who is becoming more and more impressed & convinced against his own reason.}

Fade into

Leader
"Some years after my Mother died, my Father married again. My

stepmother was not unkind, but had no real affection for me. I was happy at School, for there I ~~found the best & sweetest friend~~ became the intimate friend of the best & sweetest girl I have ever known—Evelyn Heseltine."

Return to (1). As Stella continues, *Fade out & into*

(2)

Scene The Garden of a Girls' School. In front, a bench under shady trees. At back, a court where four girls are playing tennis. Others looking on.

Action Stella & Evelyn Heseltine are sitting together on the bench. They are in summer frocks & wear straw hats with the same school ribbon as all the others. [111] Their apparent age is about 18 & they wear their hair tied in a bow at the back, as schoolgirls do. Evelyn is fair, extremely lovely, with a gentle & innocent expression, but not insipidly good. Stella is dark, handsome & spirited. A small girl comes up with some question. Stella, annoyed at being interrupted, orders the child away imperiously. Evelyn smiles, remonstrates, calls the child back & listens patiently to what she has to say. The child runs off, after kissing Evelyn impulsively. Stella looks ~~angry~~ jealous & sulky. Evelyn coaxes her out of her ~~ill-temp~~ ill-humour, & makes her laugh at herself for having been so foolish.

Fade into

Leader
"Evelyn left School before I did. Her heart was not strong, & she was ordered to go abroad. At first we wrote to one another frequently, then less often—till at last we lost touch altogether. I had been living at home for about two years, when one day my ~~father~~ stepmother told me that my Father had lost most of his money through the failure of a bank."

Fade into

(3)

Scene The Morning-Room of a Country-house.

Action A middle-aged placid-looking woman is speaking very seriously to Stella, who is listening with repressed emotion, & finally seems to have come to a sudden decision.

Fade into

Leader

"I decided that I would not remain a useless burden at home, but go out into the world & earn my own living. So I wrote to my old schoolmistress."

Fade into

(4)

Scene A bedroom with writing-table at foot of bed or by window.

Action Stella at table writing letter.

Cut in portion of letter

"So, if, dear Mʳˢ· Chichester, you happen to know of anyone who wants a governess or companion, it would be very kind of you to recommend me."

[112]

Fade into

Leader

"Soon after Mʳˢ· Chichester received my letter, she had a visit from Evelyn Heseltine, who was now recovered. Evelyn told her of her wish to find a companion of her own age, & Mʳˢ· Chichester supported me."

Fade into

(5)

Scene Mʳˢ· Chichester's Study at the School.

Action Mʳˢ· Chichester, an elderly dignified handsome woman, is at her writing bureau when Evelyn Heseltine is announced. Evelyn comes in, charmingly dressed in a costume which shows that she has come in a motor-car. Mʳˢ· C. receives her with affection. They sit down and talk. Mʳˢ· C. produces a letter, which she shows to Evelyn, who expresses enthusiastic delight.

Fade into

Leader
"And so it was all arranged. Evelyn met me at the station, & even before she spoke, I knew she loved me as dearly as ever."

Fade into

(6)

Scene A Country railway platform.
Action Evelyn waiting for train. Train arrives. Stella gets out of carriage, comes towards Evelyn a little hesitatingly & doubtfully. Evelyn embraces her ~~affectionately~~ warmly. Stella is touched & grateful. Looks admiringly at Evelyn, as if congratulating her on recovering her health & strength so completely. Evelyn laughingly declares that she is perfectly well now. She gives directions to a porter who is putting Stella's trunk on a barrow, & she & Stella go off, talking with gaiety & animation, delighted to be renewing the old friendship.

Fade into

(7)

Scene A Country road in Summer.
Action Stella & Evelyn are in a motor-car, talking & laughing. Stella looking intensely happy & thankful.

Fade into

[113]

(8)

Scene Before the porch of a small but charming old Tudor house.
Action The Car drives up. Stella and Evelyn get out. Evelyn takes her into the house.

Fade into

(9)

Scene A pretty bedroom, with a long low latticed window, chintz curtains, a Sheraton dressing-table, on which stands a vase of roses. Comfortable chintz-covered couch, writing-table, armchair &c. {View of garden, with whiplash fountain on lawn, old cedar with circular seat round trunk, through open windows, if this can be done. If not, suggestion in backing to window, of lawn & garden & trees.}

Action Evelyn brings Stella into the room, intimates that she is to consider the house her home for the future, kisses her affectionately & goes out. Stella sinks into chair, looking after Evelyn with an expression of intense gratitude & ~~devotion~~ affection.

Fade into

Leader
"Evelyn introduced me to her aunt, M^rs. Maitland, who acted as her chaperon."

Fade into

(10)

Scene A pleasant old-fashioned drawing-room with window opening on lawn. Tea-table laid.

Action Evelyn presents Stella to M^rs. Maitland, a comfortable kindly-looking widow of about 50, who receives her with friendly sympathy. Stella is still somewhat shy, but gradually reassured, and made to feel at home.

Fade into

Leader
"For some weeks I was perfectly happy. Evelyn and I were constantly together."

Fade into

(11)

Scene A Common.

Action Evelyn & Stella are walking together, with a handsome collie [114] in attendance. Evelyn caresses the dog, which is violently devoted to her. {n.b. This should be clearly shown, as it is of importance to the sequel.}

Fade into

(12)

Scene Downs, from which there is a wide view.
Action Evelyn & Stella canter up on horseback, & stop to enjoy the scenery. The Collie is with them.

(13)

Scene The lawn of a Country-house.
Action There is a Garden-party. Guests in country clothes or tennis flannels. Evelyn appears with Stella, is effusively welcomed by hostess, introduces Stella to various people, all of whom are friendly & some cordial. Stella responds, but her manner is slightly cold and reserved.

Fade into

(14)

Scene Outside a cottage.
Action Evelyn & Stella arrive in motor. Evelyn gets out, takes basket from car, & goes up path to cottage. She invites Stella to come with her, but Stella laughingly shakes her head & remains in the car.

Fade into

(15)

Scene Bedroom in cottage.
Action Cottager's wife is ill in bed. Evelyn comes in, cheers her up, & leaves parcels &c. with cottager's daughter, & goes out.

Fade into

[115]
Leader
"I thought that this peaceful life would continue, that nothing & no one could ever come between Evelyn & me. But one afternoon Hugh Dallas rode over to see her."

Fade into

(16)

Scene A Garden-lawn. Evelyn, Stella & Mrs. Maitland are sitting under a fine cedar-tree. Evelyn is in a hammock, Stella & Mrs. Maitland in wicker chairs. Stella is reading aloud, Mrs. Maitland doing some embroidery. A maid comes out of the house, followed by Hugh Dallas in riding dress. Evelyn gets out of the hammock & goes towards him. They meet as old friends who are glad to see one another again. Evelyn talks eagerly to him, while they stand at some distance from Stella & Mrs. Maitland, who whispers confidentially in Stella's ear. Stella's expression indicates jealousy & prejudice against Dallas.

Fade into

Leader

"Evelyn & Hugh Dallas, I was told, had met abroad, & Mrs. Maitland hinted that they were on terms of more than ordinary friendship. If so, it was strange that Evelyn who, I thought, told me everything, had never mentioned his name … And now I must see myself gradually supplanted!"

Fade into

(17)

Scene (continued)

Action Evelyn comes forward with Dallas, who greets Mrs. Maitland. Evelyn introduces him to Stella, who is cold & distant to him. He makes efforts to overcome this, but at length she turns from him as if bored beyond endurance, & strolls away. He looks at Evelyn with an air of asking what he has done to offend this disdainful young woman. Evelyn seems to be making excuses for Stella. Dallas sits down, but from time to time his eyes wander in the direction Stella has taken.

Fade into

[116]

Leader

"Hugh Dallas came over almost daily after that, & each time we met I loved him more deeply. But I let him think that I disliked him, for I knew too well that it was Evelyn he cared for—not me."

Fade into

(18)

Scene A walk between flowerbeds.
Action Dallas & Evelyn are strolling together, & talking intimately. Behind is Stella, with a basket & a pair of garden scissors; she lingers, snipping off dead roses &c. Dallas apparently suggests to Evelyn that they should wait for her. She comes up. He makes some friendly remark to her with a smile, & offers to relieve her of the basket. She declines with icy indifference & passes on. He looks pained & puzzled by her evident hostility. Evelyn seems to be assuring him that it is merely Stella's manner, & that she will relent in time. But Evelyn herself looks distressed & anxious.

Fade into

(19)

Scene A summer-house.
Action Stella has flung herself down on seat, sobbing with shame & despair. Presently she sits up, as if she had just resolved on some action.

Fade into

Leader
"Why, I thought, should I go on enduring a misery which I might escape whenever I chose? If I could only find some painless way of ending my life!"

Fade into

(20)

Scene A library.
Action Stella has taken down a volume from a shelf & is turning over the pages. Suddenly she stops at a passage which she reads attentively.
Cut in close-up of extract "Chloral ~~is a hypnotic which~~ should only be used ~~as~~ with the greatest caution in ~~procuring sleep~~ cases of

sleeplessness, [117] and never where there is any reason to suspect weakness of the heart. Fatal accidents from its indiscriminate use are far from uncommon."

Action (continued) Stella closes the book & puts it back with an air of having made up her mind.

Fade into

(21)

Scene The Marketplace of a small country town.

Action Motorcar stops before a grocer's or saddler's. Evelyn & Stella get out of the car. Evelyn seems to expect that Stella will come into the shop with her, but she declines, intimating that she has a purchase to make elsewhere. Evelyn, again hurt by Stella's altered manner, lets her go, & enters the shop alone.

Fade into

(22)

Scene Exterior of Chemist's shop. Name over shop. D. Wilson.

Action Stella approaches & goes in.

Fade into

(23)

Scene Interior of shop. An elderly & fatherly Chemist is behind the counter.

Action Stella comes in & asks for a particular drug. He seems to be asking her why she requires it, & she to be explaining that she suffers from sleeplessness. He tries to persuade her against taking any drug as a remedy, but, as she insists, he gives way, produces a book in which she has to write her name & address, which she does. He then shows her a small phial, with cork in kid cover.

Insert close-up of phial, a dark corrugated bottle, with printed label.

D. Wilson, Chemist. (*printed*)
Solution of Chloral. (*in pen & ink*)
3 to 6 drops to be taken in water.

Above this, another narrow label with the printed word 'Poison.'
Action (continued)
The Chemist wraps up & seals the bottle, hands it to Stella, who pays & puts bottle in her hand-bag. Chemist warns her once more, as she goes out with a smiling assurance to him that she will be careful not to exceed the proper dose.
[118]

Fade into

Leader
"I meant to take the chloral that very night, but——"

(24)

Scene Stella's Bedroom.
Action Stella, wearing a kimono, is standing beside her dressing-table. She has the packet containing the phial in her hand. She slowly tears off the paper, when she starts as though she has heard a knock at her door. She says 'come in,' & M^rs. Maitland enters. M^rs. Maitland has come to bring Stella a magazine or paper. She notices the bottle, which Stella has hastily put down on the table. Stella, taking up the bottle in such a way as to hide the word 'Poison,' laughingly reassures her. The stuff is perfectly harmless—she hasn't been sleeping well lately, & has bought it in case she has another bad night. M^rs. Maitland appears satisfied, looks at directions, cautions Stella to be careful about the number of drops, kisses her, & goes out.

Fade into

Leader
"And then I felt that I could not die till I had seen Hugh again— I did not even know for certain that he & Evelyn were actually engaged. I would wait at least till I heard that."

Fade into

Action (continued)
Stella puts the phial, unopened, in a drawer of her dressing-table.

Fade out & into

Leader
The Next Evening. After Dinner.

(25)

Scene In the Garden.

Action Stella, in foreground, is seated on circular bench under the cedar. On the lawn behind Evelyn is pacing up & down with Hugh Dallas; he seems to be pleading his cause earnestly. She listens, but her glances at Stella imply that Stella must decide. Stella meanwhile sits alone in suspense.—Evelyn & Dallas come to her. [119] She braces herself to hear news of their engagement. Evelyn leaves them together with a glance of encouragement to Hugh. He sits on bench by Stella's side. She draws slightly away from him. He appeals to her. What has he done that she should treat him as an enemy? Cannot she bring herself to look on him as her friend? If not, she has only to say so & he will leave the place.

Fade into

Leader

"I said that Evelyn had no right to leave the decisions to me. She will be willing enough to marry you when I am gone. And I shall not care—do you understand that? It is nothing to me, so long as I never see you again!"

Action (continued)

He rises, seeming to understand at least that her dislike to him is unconquerable. Then he bows coldly & leaves her. She sits on, staring in front of her, leaning forward, her chin resting on her folded hands.

Fade into

Leader

"Yet, wretched as I was, I no longer thought of killing myself. I would go on living,—if only to prove that Evelyn's scruples were insincere. It was some time before I went in, & then——"

Fade into

(26)

Scene The Drawing-room.

Action Evelyn is lying on a sofa, looking rather exhausted, but rises as Stella comes in through the French window. Stella is in a state of suppressed rage. Evelyn tries to induce her to think more kindly of Hugh. Stella declines to listen. Evelyn persists. Stella stops her ears. Evelyn catches her wrists, & draws her hands away, insisting on her explanation being heard. At this Stella wrenches [120] herself free with such violence that Evelyn staggers back & falls on the couch, lying there terrified while Stella stands over her blazing with anger. Then Stella signs to her to go before she has tempted her beyond all self-control. Evelyn rises unsteadily, looks imploringly at Stella, draws a long gasping sigh, puts her hand to her left side, & then, supporting herself on her way by chairs & couches, goes slowly out of the room. Stella stands, impenitent and stony, feeling that all is over between them.

Fade into

Leader
"I knew I had betrayed my secret. Some day she would tell him, & he would despise & pity me!"

Fade into

(27)

Scene Evelyn's Bedroom.
Action Evelyn, looking ill & exhausted, is at her writing-table, writing a letter which seems to be a difficult one to write. M^rs. Maitland enters & is alarmed by Evelyn's looks, urges her to put off writing & go to bed. Evelyn replies that she must finish her letter, & indicates that something has happened which will prevent her from sleeping that night. M^rs. Maitland looks at her anxiously & goes out.

Fade into

(28)

Scene as in (26).
Action Stella is now lying on a couch absorbed in her thoughts, but half rises as M^rs. Maitland comes in. M^rs. M. tells her something & apparently asks a question, which Stella answers. M^rs. M. thanks her again & goes out.

Fade into

Leader
"Mrs. Maitland came down to tell me that Evelyn was very upset
& excited. She was trying to write a letter—to Mr. Dallas, M^{rs.}
Maitland believed—& she would get no sleep unless she took
a sedative. Could I tell her where she could find that harmless
sleeping draught I had? So I told her."

Fade out

[121]

(29)

Scene Stella's bedroom.
Action Mrs. Maitland enters, turns on electric light, goes to
dressing-table, opens drawer & takes out the bottle. As she looks
at the directions, the word 'Poison' catches her eye. She looks
alarmed & rather doubtful, then turns off light & goes out with
the phial.

Fade into

(30)

Scene Evelyn's bedroom.
Action She finishes her letter, rises & goes out with the letter.

Fade into

(31)

Scene Stella's bedroom-door.
Action Evelyn knocks timidly, waits, receives no answer, tries
handle, finds door unlocked & goes in.

Fade into

(32)

Scene Stella's bedroom.
Action Evelyn enters, finds room unoccupied, turns on light, goes
to dressing-table, & puts the letter in a conspicuous place on the
table.
Insert close-up of envelope addressed

To my dearest Stella

Action (continued) Evelyn looks sadly at the letter, as if she fears that Stella may refuse even to read it, then she turns off the light & goes out.

Fade into

(33)

Scene Evelyn's bedroom.

Action Her maid has just seen her into bed, & is apparently asking if there is anything she can do. Evelyn, evidently worn out, smiles, indicates that the maid can go, says goodnight, then closes her eyes. The maid watches her for a moment, & then, satisfied that she is fast asleep, turns off the light & goes.

Fade into

(34)

Leader

"I myself was worn out. I fell asleep in the Drawing-room. It was early morning when I awoke, & remembered."

[122]

Scene The Drawing-room. Stella is on the couch. A lighted lamp & a small clock are on a table near her, but the sky is light outside the French window.

Action She wakes, sits up on couch, shivers in the chill morning air, looks at clock, the hands of which are at 3.30. As her thoughts become clearer, her expression shows past shame, & remorse at her treatment of Evelyn, then sudden terror.

Leader

"Evelyn had a weak heart—& I had allowed M^rs. Maitland to give her chloral!"

Action (continued) Stella rushes from Drawing-room.

Fade into

(35)

Scene Evelyn's Bedroom.

Action Stella enters & tends anxiously over Evelyn, who is lying peacefully asleep.

Fade into

Leader
"What a fool I had been to be frightened! I thought. The chloral had done her good & no harm. I went to my own room, & there I found——"

Fade into

(36)

Scene Stella's Bedroom.
Action Stella enters & goes to her dressing-table, sees the envelope, takes it up & reads the address. At first her face hardens, she seems on the point of tossing the letter away unread, but eventually she opens it, though with a slightly contemptuous smile. As she reads, her expression changes to surprise, relief, & overwhelming joy.

Cut in portion of letter

Are you blind, Stella, that you cannot see that Hugh loves you, & only you? To me he has never been, can never be, more than a friend. He is in despair at your coldness, but I made him promise to come over tomorrow. Now I know your real feelings, I can encourage him to try once more. Now good night, dearest, love me always, & never, never have bad thoughts about me again!

Evelyn

[123]
Action (continued) Stella bursts into tears, kisses the letter repeatedly, reads it again & again with rapture. Then she rises impulsively, puts the letter down on table, & goes towards the door.

Fade into

Leader
"I felt I must go to her at once. If she was still sleeping, I would sit by her till she awoke."

Fade into

(37)

Scene Evelyn's Bedroom.
Action Stella smiles softly. Evelyn is lying in the same attitude as before. Stella takes a chair by the bedside, & sits, watching her lovingly. Suddenly she becomes alarmed; she listens for Evelyn's breathing, can hear nothing. Then she touches Evelyn's hand & starts. She goes to the window & pulls up the blind. The room is flooded with light. She returns to the bed, bends over Evelyn, raises her gently, finds the body passive & lifeless, lets it sink back on the pillows, & turns away in an agony of grief.

Fade into

Leader
"Nothing would wake her any more, no words of love or gratitude would ever reach her now. Evelyn was dead."

Fade out

End of Part I

[124]

PART II

Close up of first scene
Action Stella in bed; the doctor expressing sympathy, & evidently moved by her story. She indicates that there is more to be told, & continues.

Fade into

Leader
"My first thought was to rouse the house & send for doctors—but what could they do now? Only Heaven could give me back my dead,—& Heaven might answer my prayer. And then I prayed, prayed that a miracle might happen, as of old."

Fade into

(38)

Scene Evelyn's Bedroom.

Action Stella kneeling by the bed in passionate prayer. Presently she rises, bends over Evelyn once more, & turns away, facing spectators, in wild revolt & despair.

Fade into

(39)

Leader

"Since Heaven had no mercy on me, I besought any Power that would hear me,—good or evil, angel or devil,—to aid me now and make that which was dead alive!"

Action (continued) As Stella stands in foreground, in an attitude of wild invocation, her lips moving in passionate prayer, & her arms extended, a dark shadowy form appears behind her, the form of a very beautiful woman with an evil sensuous face, whose features do not resemble Evelyn's in any way. Unseen by Stella, the form approaches the bed & looks at Evelyn critically. Then it appears to be satisfied, sinks down on the bed & gradually disappears, seeming to merge into the body of the dead girl. At the moment this happens, Stella's manner shows a sudden reaction, as though she were overcome with horror at such a prayer. She makes a gesture of repentance & submission, & kneels by the bed, her face hidden in her hands.

[125]

Leader

"Humbly I implored pardon for my impious prayer, & resigned myself to the will of heaven."

Fade into

(40)

Scene Evelyn's Bedroom.

Action Stella still kneeling. Evelyn's eyes slowly open; she raises herself slightly & looks at Stella with a cold curiosity, as though she were wondering who Stella is & how she comes to be there. Then she stretches out her right hand & touches Stella's shoulder. Stella raises her head, is paralysed for a moment, then folds the supposed Evelyn in her arms, laughing & sobbing hysterically as she covers her with kisses. Evelyn submits passively, &, as Stella grows calmer, seems to be asking for an explanation.

Fade into

Leader
"At first Evelyn seemed to have no recollection of the night before. I told her of the chloral. I accused myself of being her murderess in all but deed. And gradually she understood."

Action (continued) Evelyn listens attentively; then she covers her eyes with both hands for a moment, as though to think more clearly. Then she removes her hands, which Stella seizes & caresses, while Evelyn lies back, looking at her with a faintly ironical smile. Finally she says something which evidently wounds Stella, who lets go her hands & looks at her in ~~pained~~ hurt surprise.

Fade into

Leader
"As you say, Stella," she replied, "Heaven has let me come back. To save you from a situation that might have been rather unpleasant. How considerate of—Heaven,—& how much more careful you will be of me in future!"

Action (continued) Stella rises suddenly & looks as if she had just been struck. Evelyn laughs, heartlessly, but not with any actual ill-nature. Then, with a languid gesture, she dismisses Stella, who goes out with a dazed bewildered look.

Fade out & into

[126]
Leader "But I felt sure that Evelyn was not yet herself. I was told that she did not even recognise M^rs. Maitland when she first came in that morning."

Fade into

(41)

Scene Evelyn's bedroom.

Action Evelyn is still in bed, when M^rs. Maitland enters with a tray, on which are coffee, eggs, slices of toast in a rack, &c. Evelyn directs her, as she might a servant, to bring up a small table & put the tray on that. M^rs. M. obeys, a little surprised at her reception. Evelyn, without taking any further notice of her, begins to eat & drink, daintily enough, but with evident hunger & enjoyment. Then M^rs. M. says something which apparently enlightens Evelyn as to their relationship. She apologises with a charming smile, & offers her cheek to be kissed. After which she seems to be drawing out the unsuspicious lady & gathering useful information. M^rs. M. kisses her & goes out. Evelyn looks after her, & makes a slight grimace of amused contempt. {n.b. The change in her personality should be very subtly indicated. Her expression is no longer that of angelic goodness, but it is not openly malevolent or diabolical. The idea is that the spirit of a woman who, in her former life, was clever, unscrupulous & depraved has succeeded in animating Evelyn's dead body. This evil spirit is glad to be in comfortable surroundings, &, at present, has no animosity to Stella. It merely desires to make the most of this new life & make the best possible use of its opportunities.}

Fade into

(42)

Scene A morning-room.

Action Stella is seated in a bow-window as Evelyn comes in, radiantly lovely & looking in the best of health & spirits. Stella rises & goes towards her, impelled by the old affection & admiration. Evelyn allows herself to be embraced, & soon kisses her in return, but a little perfunctorily. Stella is slightly chilled & repelled, but seems to be reminding her of something. Evelyn expresses blank ignorance [127] of the matter. Stella takes out the letter & gives it to her.

Insert portion of letter already shown
Evelyn reads the letter with raised eyebrows & a cynical smile. Then she goes to the mantelpiece, finds a matchbox, strikes a match & sets fire to the letter, which drops blazing on to the hearth, Stella being too taken by surprise to do anything. After having burnt the letter, Evelyn turns to Stella, smiling.

Fade into

Leader
"I wonder how I could ever have written anything so sickly and sentimental," said Evelyn. "As it seems I did, I've clearly the right to destroy it. Still, I am quite willing to see Hugh Dallas & use what influence I may have over him."

Action (continued) Stella thanks her effusively. Evelyn shrugs her shoulders, as if to intimate that so trifling a service did not deserve such excessive gratitude. Stella is again repelled by the difference in her manner, but accepts the change as a just punishment.

Fade into

Leader
"When Hugh came over that afternoon———"

Fade into

(43)

Scene The Garden.
Action Evelyn & Stella are in wicker chairs under the cedar. Hugh Dallas, in riding things as before, comes towards them from the house. Evelyn & Stella rise to receive him. Stella's manner is a little conscious; she is anxious, without betraying herself, to let him see that she is no longer unfriendly. Evelyn receives him with a quiet cordiality. He scarcely seems to notice that Stella's hostility has vanished. He has no eyes but for Evelyn, whose beauty & charm have evidently struck him for the first time. She invites him carelessly to stroll round the garden with her. He eagerly accepts. They go off together. Stella remains in suspense, but evidently hoping that Evelyn will fulfil her promise.

Fade out

[128]

Leader
"Evelyn came back, alone. Hugh had gone, she told me, but he was coming back to dine, & she had great hopes of persuading him to plead his cause with me that very evening."

Action (continued) Stella rises from her chair as Evelyn approaches, seems disappointed that Hugh is not with her, till Evelyn explains, & soothes & encourages her. Stella throws her arms round Evelyn in a fervour of love & gratitude. Evelyn gently frees herself & looks at Stella with a smile of amusement which has a trace of mockery. Stella feels that she is not yet entirely forgiven.

Fade into

Leader
"After dinner that evening——"

Fade into

(44)

Scene The Drawing-room.
Action Hugh is putting a light wrap round Evelyn's shoulders. Evelyn invites Stella to come into the garden with them. Stella, knowing that the invitation is meant to be declined, intimates that she would rather stay indoors. M^rs. Maitland remains also, & takes up a book or embroidery. Hugh & Evelyn go out together. Stella sits in the window-recess, watching them as they pace up & down the lawn. From time to time M^rs. M. makes some remark & Stella answers it absently, but without turning her eyes from the garden. M^rs. M. gets up & goes out. Stella remains, expectant & hopeful that Evelyn will shortly send Hugh to her. Presently he comes in; she meets him with a shy smile. He seems relieved at the change in her manner to him, sits down by her side & begins to talk confidentially. As he goes on, her expression alters from hope to stony despair; she listens in silence, while her hands are twisting & untwisting her handkerchief.

Fade into

Leader

"Had Evelyn deceived me—or how was it that he talked only of her?"

[129]

Action (continued) Evelyn comes in. Hugh rises, & after a little conversation, says goodnight. He takes his leave of Stella with friendly cordiality, as a man might who is glad to find that a girl who had seemed antagonistic was really on his side after all, but his manner shows nothing more, & she sees this & is cut to the heart by it.

Evelyn intimates that she will see him to the front gate, & his face shows how highly he appreciates her graciousness. She goes out, laughing, with him. Stella stands with clenched hands, staring after them.

Fade out

Action (continued) Evelyn returns to the Drawing-room, smiling to herself, & moves about the room, restlessly fingering books & knick-knacks, with an occasional side-glance at Stella. Finally Stella can bear it no longer. She faces Evelyn, & seems to be demanding an explanation. Evelyn laughs & spreads her hands. "Is it her fault if Hugh prefers her to Stella?" Stella pleads with her. Evelyn replies mockingly. Stella sinks sobbing at her feet, & Evelyn seizes her wrists & draws her up, forcing her to look in her face. Stella looks, & falls in a dead faint.

Fade into

Leader

"'You fool!' she said, 'I am not the innocent trusting girl you allowed to be drugged to death! Look at me well—& you will understand!'

"And then—God help me—I understood at last!"

Fade out

End of Part II

[130]

PART III

Leader
The Next Morning.

(45)

Scene Stella's Room.
Action Stella, already dressed for a journey, is putting some things into a handbag. A trunk is seen in the background.
Evelyn enters. Stella cowers back in horror. Evelyn uses all her wiles to reassure her. She is no longer cruel & taunting, but is evidently anxious to gain Stella's confidence. She is so bewitchingly endearing that Stella finds it hard to resist her.

Fade into

Leader
"'I can't do without you, Stella,' she said. 'Stay with me & I can make you love me better than you ever loved Evelyn. Tell me we are to be allies!'"
Action (continued) Stella gradually gives way, though against her better judgment. Evelyn kisses her triumphantly, makes her take off her hat & gloves, & then leaves her. Stella, in shame at having surrendered, sinks into chair, hiding her face in her hands.

Fade into

(46)

Scene Outside the Stables.
Action An elderly coachman is in his shirtsleeves, carrying a bucket of water. Evelyn's collie is seen fastened to his kennel by a stout chain. Evelyn & Stella appear. The coachman's face lights up with affectionate admiration as he touches his forehead to Evelyn. The collie comes forward wagging his tail. Evelyn evidently has to ask Stella the names both of the coachman & dog. Stella prompts her quietly. As Evelyn comes nearer the dog's manner changes, he bristles, & retreats growling.
Close up of the dog in a state of fury, straining at his chain, & bark-

ing madly. Evelyn has started back, & stands at a safe distance, looking both frightened & angry.

[131]

The Coachman tries to soothe the dog, & warns Evelyn & Stella to keep at a distance. Stella drags Evelyn away.

Fade into

Leader

"The dog knows!" I told her. "What is the use of *my* being silent. You will never silence *him*!"

"When you see him next,' she said, 'he will be quiet enough."

Fade into

(47)

Scene The stable yard.

Action Evelyn returns alone. The dog becomes furious as before. Keeping well away from him, she gives the coachman instructions. ~~Reynolds~~ He receives them sorrowfully. Evelyn affects pity for the dog. He goes into harness-room.

Fade into

(48)

Close up of interior of Harness-room. On a shelf is a bottle labelled 'Prussic Acid.' He is seen taking down the bottle.

(49)

Scene The Shrubbery.

Action The Coachman is digging a grave. By the side of the half-dug grave lies the dog's dead body. Stella comes by, stops in sudden horror as she sees it, asks for explanations from the Coachman, who gives them reluctantly. She passes on. He brushes his eyes with his hand, & then goes on digging the grave.

Fade into

(50)

{n.b. This will be effective if it can be carried out, but if this is not practicable it can be omitted.}

Scene Outside the front gate, or on the drive before the house.

Action Hugh is waiting on horseback. Evelyn & Stella come out dressed for riding. He dismounts & talks to them. Evelyn's manner is very gay & animated. The Coachman & a groom appear, leading two horses saddled for riding outside. Evelyn is about to mount, when her horse plunges & rears & becomes almost uncontrollable. [132] Evelyn, though evidently disconcerted, seems determined to ride. Hugh takes it on himself to dissuade her. Her mare is vicious, he insists that Evelyn shall not risk her life on such a brute. Evelyn consents, with a charming smile in acknowledgment of his care for her safety. The three horses are led away. Evelyn & Hugh go indoors together, she leaning slightly on his arm. Stella stands for a moment; then, with a look of pity for Hugh's infatuation & her own powerlessness, she follows them.

Fade into

(51)

Leader

"It must have been the next day, that Evelyn told me Hugh had asked her to be his wife—& she had consented."

Scene The Library.

Stella is in a chair, absorbed in a volume.

Vignette to show title of volume. 'Letters on Demonology & Witchcraft. Scott.'

Open to full screen

Action Evelyn steals in; as soon as Stella is aware of her, she hastily conceals the volume. Evelyn affects not to notice this. She leans over Stella with a pretty shyness & tells her of her engagement. Stella recoils in horror & indignation. Evelyn looks plaintive & bewildered. Stella rises, & seems to be threatening to denounce her if she does not break this engagement. Evelyn throws off the mask & cynically defies her.

Fade into

Leader

"'Tell him what you please,' she said. 'Hugh will not believe you. He will only think you have gone mad—for love of him! So, in your own interests, I should advise you to say nothing!'"

Action (continued) Stella realises once more that she is powerless & indicates that she submits. Evelyn laughs, gives her a little butterfly kiss[5] on the forehead, & goes out. Stella takes up the book, looks at it for a moment, then puts it aside with a shudder, & prays fervently.

Fade out & into

[133]

(52)

Scene In the Garden.

Action Stella is sitting alone under the Cedar. Hugh Dallas comes towards her, carrying a Pekinese spaniel under one arm. He greets Stella cordially, seems to be asking where Evelyn is, explains that he has brought the dog as a gift for her. Stella loses all command of herself, & speaks with a violence that evidently surprises & shocks him. At this moment Evelyn appears behind.

Fade into

Leader

"'M^r. Dallas,' I said, 'I warn you. Don't give that dog to her. If you do, it will not live long!'"

Action (continued) Evelyn comes forward, looking alarmed, gently lays her hand on Stella's arm & tries to restrain her. Stella shakes her off, &, with another gesture of passionate warning to Hugh & horror of Evelyn, leaves them. Evelyn sweetly makes excuses for Stella, explains that she has been strange & excited of late, affects to be anxious & sorry about her, & sheds a few tears. He is touched by her sorrow, seems to be suggesting that she should send Stella away. Evelyn refuses, indicates that she could not be so unkind—she must bear with her. He embraces her, full of admiration for her goodness. Hugh has put the dog down on the lawn, but he now picks it up & offers it to Evelyn, who expresses the greatest gratitude & delight. {If it can be contrived that the dog should struggle & eventually make its escape from her, it would be an effective detail. If not, Evelyn must put it down on the seat as soon as possible & take no further notice of it. The dog should then scamper off in the direction Stella has taken.}

Fade out & into

[134]

(53)

Scene The Hall, with panelled walls, & the foot of a wide staircase. *Action* Stella is coming downstairs, when the little Pekinese dog approaches. It comes up to her as if appealing for protection. Struck with pity, she takes it up in her arms, & carries it up the stairs.

Fade into

Leader "Late that night I was sitting in my room, when———"

(54)

Scene Stella's bedroom.
Action Stella is in an armchair, thinking, with her chin resting on one hand. The dog is lying on her lap, asleep. The door behind her opens, & Evelyn enters. Stella looks around & forbids her with a gesture to come nearer. Evelyn, seeming pained by her distrust, advances pleadingly. Stella remains on her guard for a time, but gradually, overcome by Evelyn's soft words, is won over to some extent. She shudders under Evelyn's caresses, but she submits to them. Evelyn strokes the dog, & Stella allows her to take it from her. Evelyn clasps the dog to her breast, & turns away, with her back to Stella. Presently she turns again, & with a cruel & triumphant laugh flings the body of the dog, which she has just strangled, into Stella's lap. Stella rises, her expression conveying that Evelyn has over-reached herself, & goes towards the bell-rope. As she is putting out her hand to ring & denounce Evelyn, Evelyn stops her, & says something maliciously at which Stella cowers back in terror.

Fade into

(55)

Leader
"'Ring by all means,' she said. 'I shall have to say that I came in just too late to save the poor creature. Who will take your word against mine? Remember your warning to Hugh! He will think, like everyone else, that you are mad with love & jealousy. But if you choose to say tomorrow that the dog had a fit & died during the night, I promise to be guileless enough to believe you!'"
[135]
Action (continued) Evelyn smiles again, gives Stella a careless little nod, & goes out. Stella crouches over the dog's body in an agony of despair.

Fade into

Leader The Next Morning.

(56)

Scene The Entrance Hall.
Action Hugh has ridden over as usual. Evelyn is welcoming him affectionately as Mrs. Maitland & Stella come down the stairs. Hugh asks Evelyn a question. She refers him to Stella. She answers his question in evident confusion & distress. Evelyn & Mrs. Maitland express surprise & concern. Hugh looks at Stella coldly & keenly for a moment or two, & she hides her face in her hands. Then in stern disgust he turns away from her, & draws Evelyn with him towards the garden. Mrs. Maitland regards Stella wonderingly, as she goes slowly upstairs, supporting herself by the handrail.

Fade out

End of Part III

[136]

PART IV

Leader
"She would not have let me go, even if I had wished to—& I did

not. I felt sure that Hugh would discover the truth before long, & return to me. She had given up attending Church, so neither of them was present on the Sunday when their banns were published for the third time."

Fade into

(57)

Scene The Chancel of a Village Church.
Close-up of a dignified elderly clergyman in a surplice, reading from a paper in his hand. Suddenly his expression changes to consternation & severe disapproval.

Fade into

(58)

Scene Section of Nave. M^rs. Maitland & Stella are the only occupants of a large pew. Other members of the congregation in pews at the back. All are sitting down. Suddenly Stella rises; she is perfectly calm & intensely earnest as she speaks. The others start in surprise & dismay.

Fade into

Leader
"'I forbid the banns,' I said. 'I know of a reason why this marriage would be unholy in the sight of Heaven—& I am ready to declare it.'"

Fade into

(58)[6]

Scene Close-up as in (57).
Action The Clergyman orders her to be silent, & intimates that he will see her after the service.

Fade into

(59)

Scene A Vestry. Churchman's Almanack on Wall. Surplices &c.

hanging up—the Rector has taken off his surplice & is seated at a table. Mᴿˢ· Maitland, looking very nervous & flurried, enters with Stella, who is still composed. At a sign from the Rector Mᴿˢ· Maitland withdraws, & he intimates to Stella that, although she has acted wrongly in disturbing the service, he is ready to hear her. He warns her first against making any charges she cannot [137] prove. {n.b. This of course cannot be expressed in dumb-show; it is enough that he should seem to be reproving & warning her.} She then tries to tell him the facts, growing more & more vehement as she goes on. He listens, shielding his eyes with one hand, till she has finished. Then he looks at her with pity, rises, goes to door & summons Mᴿˢ· Maitland. She enters, & he gives Stella into her charge.

Fade into

(60)

Scene At the Lych-gate of the Church.
Action The Rector, bareheaded, has come down the path with Mᴿˢ· Maitland & Stella, & opens the gate for them. Stella turns & makes a parting speech, in reply to which he shakes his head compassionately.

Fade into

Leader
"'I am indeed, as you say, to be pitied,' I told him, 'when you, who claim to represent Heaven here, will do nothing to deliver me from the power of Hell!'"

Fade into

(61)

Scene The Lawn.
Action Hugh is seated by Evelyn, looking at her admiringly as she talks. Mᴿˢ· Maitland comes towards them, evidently agitated & flurried, & describes the scene in Church. Evelyn is distressed, Hugh indignant. Stella now joins them. She is excited & defiant, denounces Evelyn, who shrinks back, & tries to calm her. Stella is reckless. She again warns Hugh, who has stepped forward to pro-

tect Evelyn from one whom he supposes to be a madwoman. M^rs. Maitland puts her arms round Stella & leads her away. After she has gone, Hugh urges Evelyn once more to have Stella sent home or put under restraint. Evelyn refuses, with an air of angelic patience. Stella is more likely to recover here than anywhere else, she urges. It would be cruel to send her away.

[138]

In his admiration for her goodness he lifts both her hands & kisses them reverently. As he bends his head she smiles down on him with a coldly amused contempt.

Fade out

(62)

Leader

The Night before the Wedding.

Scene Stella's Bedroom.

Action Stella is lying in bed, staring into space with hopeless eyes. The door is gently opened & Evelyn enters. She is wearing her bridal dress & puts back her veil as she approaches, looking radiantly lovely. Stella turns & looks at her as though fascinated. Evelyn sits on the bed, pinions Stella's shoulders so that she cannot raise her hands to her ears, &, crouching over her, whispers malignantly, while Stella writhes in helpless terror & agony of mind.

Fade into

Leader

"She told me that she hated Hugh for having once loved me. She gloried in the misery she would make him endure. She taunted me with the madhouse, where I should soon be a prisoner. There were many other things she said, so horrible that I dare not repeat them."

Fade into

Leader

On the Wedding Day.

"As I sat at a window, dreading to hear the bells ring out, & still no sound reached me, I felt a sudden hope. Might not the evil spirit that had taken the place of my beloved Evelyn have betrayed itself at the final moment? If so, Hugh was saved! And presently, as I looked out, I saw——"

(63)

Scene A view of the front garden & gate, as seen from an upper window.

Action A carriage & pair of white horses has stopped before the gate. The coachman's whip is adorned with a white favour, & he & the footman wear white flowers in their coats. [139] Hugh goes out, looking proud & happy, helps Evelyn, who is radiant & smiling, to descend, & they go up the path together, as the carriage moves on & another comes up.

Fade into

(64)

Vignette Stella at the window, laughing wildly & hysterically, violently thrown off her mental balance.

Fade into

Leader
Two Hours Later.

(65)

Scene The Entrance Hall.

Action Evelyn, in her going-away costume, & Hugh, in a travelling suit, are saying goodbye to a few intimate friends, all laughing & talking, expressing good wishes, &c.

Then there is a general embarrassment as Stella descends the stairs. Evelyn looks alarmed, but forces herself to speak pleasantly to her. Hugh offers her his hand. Stella looks at them with piteous eyes & a vacant smile, as though she were trying to remember who they were. Then, as if the effort was hopeless, she shakes her head, turns & goes away. M^rs. Maitland, after a hurried talk with Evelyn & Hugh, who seems to be entrusting Stella to her care, follows Stella. Evelyn sighs, then smiles brightly, as Hugh looks at his watch & tells her they have no time to lose.

They go out, in a shower of rose-leaves, confetti, &c.

Fade out & into

Leader

"I remember nothing of the weeks that followed—till one day, when I was recovering, good M^rs. Maitland tried to prove to me that I had nothing whatever to reproach myself with, as she had not given Evelyn the chloral after all."

Scene Stella's room.

Action Stella, as an invalid, is in an armchair, with a shawl or wrap round her shoulders. M^rs. Maitland is showing her the phial, & pointing out that the cover is still round the cork. Stella listens & seems to be convinced & relieved.

Fade into

[140]

Leader

"I let her think that she had convinced me. But nothing could alter the fact that Evelyn had died, & another had taken her form, in answer to my wicked prayer."

Fade into

(66)

Scene The Garden. Stella & M^rs. Maitland are sitting under a tree. It is Autumn. From time to time, a leaf flutters down on the grass at their feet. The lawn & path are strewn thickly with dead leaves. A maid comes out with a letter, which she gives Stella, who opens it quietly & reads.

Cut in portion of letter in female hand

Now you are quite well again, dearest, you must come over to Laleham for a few days. Hugh has been very unhappy about me lately. I believe he has taken it into his head that he sees a change in me. Of course he is wrong, & you must help me to reassure him.

Ever your loving

Evelyn Dallas.

Action (continued) Stella calmly shows the letter to M^rs. Maitland. M^rs. Maitland seems to be doubtful about the wisdom of accepting, but Stella declares that she is quite recovered, & that she intends to go.

Fade into

Leader
"When I arrived at Laleham Court, Hugh was there to receive me, & I could see in his eyes that he was, if possible, suffering even worse torment than mine."

Fade into

(67)

Scene A panelled Library.
Action Hugh, looking grave & anxious, like a man oppressed by a hidden dread, is facing Stella with an air of inquiry, as though asking whether she can trust herself to meet his wife. She looks at him with intense pity, & signifies that she is ready. He leads the way out, & she follows with [141] the air of one who has already decided what she must do.

Fade into

(68)

Scene A pleasant Jacobean or Tudor room with panelled walls, & a big Oriel window. Flowers in vases & bowls. Evelyn is lying on a sofa, as Hugh brings Stella in to see her. Evelyn half rises, & holds out her arms. Stella hesitates for a moment, then goes to her & allows herself to be kissed. Evelyn laughs & talks, seeming to be rallying Hugh on his gloomy looks. Hugh makes an effort to respond. Evelyn then dismisses him, explaining that she wishes to be alone with Stella. He seems reluctant to leave Stella, but Evelyn insists. As he is going, she calls him back & offers her cheek to be kissed. He kisses her on the forehead, closing his eyes as he does so. Then, with a haggard broken glance at Stella, as if he was still apprehensive about her safety, he goes out of the room. Stella's eyes follow him pityingly. After he has gone Evelyn rises from the sofa, & seems to be exulting in the ruin she has made of Hugh's life, & taunting Stella with her hopeless love. Stella has retreated to the door, where she quickly turns the key in the lock, extracts the key & drops it behind a cabinet close by. Then she faces Evelyn & speaks. Evelyn cowers back in evident terror.

Fade into

Leader "'If I were unable to save him from you,' I said, 'you would not be so afraid of me. But you are—& I am going to save him, if it costs me my own life!'"

Action (continued) Evelyn, her face distorted by hate & abject terror, makes a wild rush for the bell-rope. Stella cuts her off, seizes her by the throat with both hands, & forces her slowly back to the sofa, while she tries in vain to free herself.

Fade out and into

[142]

Close up Evelyn lies dead on the sofa, her face contorted & her expression evil. Stella stands gazing down on her with sombre satisfaction. A shadowy female form with the same beautiful wicked face as in (39) detaches itself from Evelyn's body, makes a wild gesture of despair & baffled malice, & disappears.

As it does so, Evelyn's face becomes innocent & calm, the lips relaxing into a gentle smile. Stella bends over her & kisses her forehead, then she crosses Evelyn's hands over her breast, takes flowers from a bowl, & lays them on the body.

Open to full screen.

Stella goes to the door, unlocks it, & passes slowly out.

Fade out and into

Scene, as in (1).

Action Stella, exhausted, has sunk back on her pillows, while the Medical Superintendent watches her with an expression of deep compassion & anxiety. She goes on speaking, but with an evident effort.

Fade into

Leader "That all happened years ago. Hugh has long been dead. But every night now I dream that he and the Evelyn I loved are alive; we are back in the old garden together, all is understood & forgiven, & the past as though it had never been. And when I fall asleep I pray that I may never awake, so that my dream will go on for ever."

Fade out and into

Scene as in (1) continued.

Stella's eyes close.

Background fades into

(69)

Scene The Garden.
Action Hugh & Stella are seated under the cedar tree. Her head is on his shoulder, his arm is round her waist. Evelyn (as she was) comes on, with the collie [143] leaping round her. Hugh & Stella greet her without changing their attitude. She puts one hand on his shoulder in a sisterly fashion as she stoops and kisses Stella.

Fade out

The End

20 : Feb : 1916

NOTES

1   In Parts Anstey leaves a space here, presumably to be filled in once the division into parts was determined. (He in fact decided on four parts, but never added that detail to the title-page.)

2   Miss Lillah McCarthy Lillah McCarthy, by now in her early forties, was a well-known actress who in 1906 had married the playwright and Shakespeare scholar Hartley Granville-Barker.

3   Miss Lydia Bilbrooke Anstey's casting again has regard more to facial features than to age. Nina Severing had passed thirty, and Lydia Bilbrook (who added the 'e' to her surname for professional purposes) was in her late twenties.

4   *Leader* A "leader" is an explanatory intertitle, or insert into a silent film. So these lines of text would be flashed up on the screen for audiences to read.

5   butterfly kiss A butterfly kiss is given with the eyelashes, not the lips.

6   (58) The second 'Scene 58' is Anstey's mistake. If it were corrected, the total number of scenes would of course rise from 69 to 70.